CW00833505

SEVENTEEN MINUTES
TO
BAKER STREET

[Being another manuscript found in the tin dispatch box of
Dr. John H. Watson
in the vault of Cox & Co., Charing Cross, London]

Book Three in the Series,
Sherlock Holmes and the American Literati

As Edited

By

Daniel D. Victor, Ph.D.

First edition published in 2016
© Copyright 2016
Daniel D. Victor

The right of Daniel D. Victor to be identified as the author of
this work has been asserted by him in accordance with the
Copyright, Designs and Patents Act 1998.

All rights reserved. No reproduction, copy or transmission of
this publication may be made without express prior written
permission. No paragraph of this publication may be
reproduced, copied or transmitted except with express prior
written permission or in accordance with the provisions of
the Copyright Act 1956 (as amended). Any person who
commits any unauthorised act in relation to this publication
may be liable to criminal prosecution and civil claims for
damage.

Although every effort has been made to ensure the accuracy
of the information contained in this book, as of the date of
publication, nothing herein should be construed as giving
advice. The opinions expressed herein are those of the
author and not of MX Publishing.

Paperback ISBN 9781780929484
ePub ISBN 978-1-78092-949-1
Mobipocket/Kindle ISBN 978-1-78092-950-7

Published in the UK by MX Publishing
335 Princess Park Manor, Royal Drive,
London, N11 3GX
www.mxpublishing.co.uk
Cover design by www.staunch.com

Also by Daniel D. Victor

The Seventh Bullet:
The Further Adventures of Sherlock Holmes

A Study in Synchronicity

The Final Page of Baker Street
(Book One in the series,
Sherlock Holmes and the American Literati)

Sherlock Holmes
and the
Baron of Brede Place
(Book Two in the series,
Sherlock Holmes and the American Literati)

Acknowledgements

I am once again greatly appreciative for all the suggestions offered to me by Norma Silverman, Seth Victor, Ethan Victor, Barry Smolin, Mark Holzband, Sylvia and Robert MacDowell, and Sandy Cohen. And a special thank you to Hamilton Hay for being so generous with his research on Mark Twain and Dollis Hill House.

I'd especially like to thank Steve Emecz for guiding me through the publication of all three books in the American Literati series. Without his help, these manuscripts might never have seen the light of day.

Here's another for Norma, Seth and Ethan

Writing is the magical possibility
that exists in the cracks of our reality.
--Walter Mosley
"Reflections on the Detective
Stories of Mark Twain . . ."

Holmes opened his eyes now and looked again at the ceiling, weighing
the problem's solution . . .
(like Dr. Watson working out the plot of a story, he reasoned—
the mixing of what was and what never had been into a single,
undeniable creation).
--Mitch Cullin
A Sleight Trick of the Mind

Maybe sometimes vengeance is just as good as justice.
--Michael Connelly
The Poet

Editor's Note

While the following manuscript appears as Dr. Watson wrote it, I have taken the liberty to give his narrative a title, separate it into sections, and introduce his chapters with what I hope are relevant headnotes from the works of Mark Twain. I should also point out that many of the witticisms expressed by Samuel Clemens and recorded by Dr. Watson may sound familiar since they have been published in various forms by Mr. Clemens himself.

D.D.V.
January 2016

Part I

Murder at Thor Bridge

Chapter One

> In one place, all by itself, stood this blood-curdling word: *"Rache!"*
> There was no name signed and no date. It was an inscription well
> calculated to pique curiosity. One would greatly like to know the nature
> of the wrong that had been done, and what sort of vengeance was
> wanted, and whether the prisoner ever achieved it or not. But there was
> no way of finding out these things.
> --Mark Twain
> *A Tramp Abroad (1880)*

"Holmes!" I cried, beginning to tremble.

The spring of '02 had prolonged the cold of winter, and there was iciness in the air. But it wasn't the chill that made me shiver that April morning. It was the unspeakable horror I felt when, upon entering our sitting room, I saw Sherlock Holmes lying limp on the sofa.

He'd obviously suffered a damaging wound. His eyes were shut, and his pallor shone a ghastly white. A badge of bright scarlet covered the lapels of his mouse-coloured dressing gown; and his left arm hung down at his side, the long, delicate fingers curling claw-like where they touched the burgundy carpet.

From the doorway, I could see that he was breathing; and I immediately rushed to his aid, opening his shirt at the collar and massaging his hands to get the blood flowing. Frightened though I was, I couldn't pretend to be shocked. Holmes often spoke of the mortal dangers he courted, and his alertness to such threats accompanied him like a faithful dog. With miscreants like Professor Moriarty and Colonel Moran vowing to get level with him—not to mention a slew of petty criminals and resentful toffs—Holmes remained ever aware of possible attacks upon his person.

"Never let your guard down, old fellow," he had cautioned me many times.

Yet clearly someone had got through his defences. Even as I ministered to him, I could hear at my back the cry for retribution that echoed throughout so many of Holmes' cases. The very first murder we investigated, the one I titled *A Study in Scarlet*, was motivated by revenge; and it might have served as a signpost for the majority of the cases that followed. One morning in early March of '81, Holmes had been summoned by Inspector Gregson to an empty house at 3, Lauriston Gardens off the Brixton Road. On a patch of yellow wall plaster not far from where a man's body had been found, the police discovered the word "*Rache*", German for "vengeance", scripted in blood. It wasn't a term that surprised Sherlock Holmes.

"There are certain crimes which the law cannot touch, Watson," he'd observed on another occasion, "and which therefore justify private revenge." How ironical that on the terrible morning when I found Holmes prostrate on the sofa, he seemed to have fallen victim to the very inattentiveness he'd warned me to avoid.

Some revenge-seeker had obviously scored a most palpable hit; and yet in spite of my searching Holmes' inert form, I could detect no signs of bodily injury. There was no physical wound. One didn't have to be a doctor to reach the singular conclusion: without such marks, the attack upon my friend—however debilitating—could only have been spiritual in nature.

"Wait a moment!" I can hear my critics complaining. "Absent an actual blade, it must follow that the scarlet on Holmes' breast cannot be real blood."

And, indeed, that was the case: there was no blood. The sanguinary image I had previously reported served to symbolize my original fears. It was, I confess, an allusion to the crimson-coloured boards of a book Holmes had let fall, pages down, to his chest. Splayed open as they were, the bright-red book covers rose and fell in accordance with the shortness of his breath. From a distance, they had looked to me like oozing collections of blood.

I was placing the deceptive volume on a nearby side-table just as Holmes' eyes fluttered open.

"You've had some sort of shock," I said, raising him up and proffering a dose of medicinal brandy. When he'd finished it, I commanded, "Now rest."

Holmes fell backward into the couch and closed his eyes again. It took but a few moments for him to fall asleep. Once I saw that he was comfortable, I resolved to satisfy my curiosity. Picking up the book, I positioned myself on the edge of the sofa and began to turn the pages. The volume wasn't long; and it didn't take much more than half an hour to complete the entire piece—time enough for me to understand how the contents of so thin a work could trigger such a catastrophic reaction in my friend.

At first glance, the narrative titled "A Double-Barrelled Detective Story" appears a simple but violent tale set in the western United States. The plot featured a heartless villain named Jacob Fuller, who near the start of the story lashes his pregnant wife to a tree and proceeds to beat her. Before fleeing, the coward sets his bloodhounds upon the poor woman, a vicious attack that leaves her naked and bloodied. It is a grim fiction, and yet in the beginning there is not a hint of the vitriol that would later be directed at my decidedly non-fictional friend.

For years, the woman nurses her hatred; and finally, after deciding that her son Archy is old enough to help, she seeks revenge against her assailant. Archy, it so happens, is an amateur detective, who *in utero* had somehow acquired the olfactory talents of the bloodhounds that attacked his mother. His search for Jacob Fuller leads to a mining camp in California where, coincidentally, a young man named Fetlock Jones has been accused of murdering a comrade.

Now occur two of the greatest coincidences in all detective literature. First, Jones' uncle turns out to be none other than Sherlock Holmes. And second, the detective—conveniently visiting the United States at the time—just happens to be touring in the vicinity. The sophisticated reader expects Holmes to free his feckless nephew by revealing the identity of the true murderer.

"Wait a moment!" I again hear my outraged audience cry. "Sherlock Holmes' *nephew*? The idea is absurd!"

Indeed, such a relation defies belief. The most casual of readers will recall that—rumours of additional siblings to the contrary—Sherlock Holmes had but one brother, the ever-pensive and generally immobile Mycroft. And among the great certainties in life must unquestionably be that the cerebral Mycroft never married—let alone, fathered a child. I myself, who can imagine fancy crime writers of the future enhancing their fictional dramas with romanticized versions of Holmes or Lestrade or even Moriarty, draw the line at energizing Mycroft Holmes.

Yet such preposterous family relationships pale in comparison with the egregious depiction of my friend and colleague in the story. Sherlock Holmes appears not as the

4

spirited and rational thinking machine he epitomizes in actuality, but rather as a moustachioed, English fop. This counterfeit detective undermines the analytical powers of the true Sherlock Holmes by wrongly building an ironclad case against one of the innocent suspects. Ultimately, the counterfeit Holmes is proven wrong and roundly ridiculed, completely humiliated, and—for good measure—almost burned to death.

In the end, it is the amateur—the opposite of a *thinking* detective, a sham of a rational investigator—who solves the case. Archy, the sleuth with the talented nose, quite literally sniffs out the true the murderer, a villain who conveniently turns out to be the long-sought attacker of Archy's mother as well. Needless to say, the young detective's success holds up to scorn the feebleness of the fictional Sherlock Holmes.

Now no victim of such spite-filled ridicule could possibly mistake this burlesque for reality—no victim, that is, with even the slightest ability to laugh at himself. But therein lay the genius of this mean-spirited ambush. A physical battering of his person Sherlock Holmes could have parried; a literary attack on his sacred methodology, his *raison d'être*, was another matter entirely. Due to his inability to tolerate the silliest of jokes at his own expense—let alone an unanticipated frontal assault on his powers of ratiocination—the real Sherlock Holmes, the cold and practical thinker, rendered himself the perfect mark for such malice.

Holmes lay devastated before me, done in by one of the most famous of metonymic adages—an observation noted in the Bible, pondered by the Greeks, immortalized by Bulwer-Lytton. Sherlock Holmes had fallen victim not to a common sword, but to the always-mightier pen.

And that wasn't the end to it. Making matters worse was

the identity of the weapon's owner, for the power of the barb might have been lessened had its author been of no account. But, alas, such was not the case. For clearly identified on the red front-cover of "A Double-Barrelled Detective Story" was the name of its creator—the pen-wielder who claimed his writing instrument had been "warmed up in hell". It wasn't some anonymous scribe who'd attacked my friend. The nemesis of Sherlock Holmes was, in fact, the most celebrated writer in the world—the sharp-tongued American author, Samuel Langhorne Clemens, whom the world has come to know by the *nom de plume* of Mark Twain.

I am no psychologist and cannot with any degree of assurance identify the emotional catalyst for Clemens' aggressive behaviour. At their initial meetings, he and Holmes appeared to have got along well. It was only later—when they tried working together to discover who'd been responsible for the deadly combination of events on Thor Bridge—that differences arose. Yet only with the arrival of Clemens' venomous text did I discover how deeply those differences had burrowed.

"A Double-Barrelled Detective Story" had appeared serially in an American magazine three months earlier, but it was not until the April morning in question that Holmes received by post the single-volume edition published by Harper and Brothers. Had he somehow been able to read a letter Clemens had written to friend and pastor Joe Twichell prior to the story's appearance, Holmes might have prepared himself. I'm sure the book's impact would have been less devastating. In the missive dated 8 September 1901, Clemens had let slip an inkling of the hostility he'd been harbouring. He described Sherlock Holmes to Twichell as "pompous" and "sentimental", as a man whose ingenuity was "cheap and ineffectual". But of all this my friend knew nothing.

In spite of the ill will Samuel Clemens directed at Sherlock

Holmes, I can safely assure my faithful readers that the basis for Clemens' antagonism was flawed from the start. From the very beginning, he'd aimed his ire at the wrong target. His anger should never have been directed at my friend; it should have been heaped upon me. After all, *I* was the one who'd followed Conan Doyle's suggestions. As my literary agent, Sir Arthur had recommended I withhold certain facts pertaining to Clemens and the events of that fateful night on Thor Bridge. Worse still, I was also the one who'd sent to Clemens the printer's proofs of the amended narrative—the same proofs, which had ignited Clemens' wrath in the first place, a hostility that not incidentally prompted me to postpone for many years the initial publication of the account.

Only now, with so many of the prominent characters having passed, do I feel comfortable enough to amend the public record with the true narrative. However much it may displease Conan Doyle, I have come to believe that it is time to acknowledge the invaluable contributions of Samuel Clemens in solving the murder on Thor Bridge. After all, what other form of apology is left to a writer—to a historian, really—than setting the record straight?

Less charitable readers may argue that my apology comes too late, and with them I am forced to agree. I can only counter that my *mea culpa* applies to peripheral mistakes in an investigation involving capital crimes. Even so, had I ignored Conan Doyle's advice or facilitated greater cooperation between Holmes and Clemens, there might have been no divisive disagreement and thus no reason for assigning blame to anyone. Yet these suppositions detract from the obvious. It would have been far simpler and far nobler had there been no murder committed on Thor Bridge for me to report in the first place.

Chapter Two

None of us can ever have as many virtues as the fountain pen,
or half its cussedness;
but we can try.
--Mark Twain
Pudd'nhead Wilson's New Calendar

In reality, the investigation I titled "The Problem of Thor Bridge" began in July of 1900—not in October, as my ill-conceived attempt to cloud the true facts purported. Nor, as I'd also recorded, did the origins of the case begin at Baker Street. I didn't realize it at the time, but the earliest clues connected to the cold-blooded killing on Thor Bridge were initially disclosed to me in the innocent confines of Nevill's Turkish Baths, the establishment in Northumberland Avenue here in London that Holmes and I often visited together.

Now I have good reason to remember the summer of 1900. Its great variations in temperature frequently aggravated my old war wound, the result of a Jezail bullet fired in Afghanistan many years before. Military training in the desert heat had prepared me for warm weather; but whenever the heat dropped in London, my shoulder would throb mercilessly. Some unfortunates suffer chronic migraines or stinging arthritis in changing weather; I was (and continue to be) tormented by warfare long past.

Attentive readers may recall that I periodically took

myself to Nevill's to gain some measure of relief from my unhappy condition. Though more recently I have been forced to add rheumatism and aging to the complaints that have driven me there, on this particular mid-summer's day the sun had chosen not to show its face, and pain shot through me in protest. Sherlock Holmes was nowhere to be seen; and in desperate need of the relief provided by concentrated heat and vigorous massage, I hailed a hansom on my own.

Jostling down Baker Street, the cab maneuvered amongst the other carriages and motorcars; and soon we were rattling past the green swards of Hyde Park and the then-honey-coloured walls of Buckingham Palace—it would be more than a decade before the familiar white Portland stone would be mounted. Finally, after negotiating some additional pockets of traffic, we reached Northumberland Avenue and were able to make our way down the road to Nevill's.

Once within, I quickly exchanged my street-clothes for a toga-like white towel and none too soon was embracing the heat. Almost immediately, I could sense my muscles relaxing, my tensions unwinding, my entire system cleansed. A cold shower followed; and soon I lay stretched out on a wooden bench thoroughly enervated and drained. Transported by the dexterous manipulations of the massage and the sweetly exotic aromas of its attendant oil, I envisioned myself at peace in some sort of desert Kasbah. Surrounded by the intoxicating scents from a nearby harem, I watched dozens of veiled beauties dance through my brain. Oh, welcome dreams! For the moment, pain and worry evaporated.

Small wonder that by the end of the session it took some effort to get up. But eventually I rose from the bench; and after securing a pair of bath slippers and another toga—this one a soft sheet of white linen—I climbed the stairs to the upper floor and Nevill's wood-panelled drying-room. With its grand high dome helping circulate the hot air and the tumbling waters of the Doulton Lambeth fountain in the centre masking the raucous sounds of the city outside, the spacious apartment presented a particularly satisfying chamber in which to cool down and embrace the lassitude.

I dozed for a few minutes, awakened, and then dozed again. But no indulgence can go on indefinitely; and after a while, feeling more like my usual self, I sat up. Normally, I would have turned to Holmes for conversation; but companionless for the day, I endeavoured to embrace my solitude. I filled my pipe with Arcadia mixture, inhaled contentedly, and surveyed my surroundings.

On the other side of the room, a group of men clad in the same white costumes as my own were engaging in animated discussion; they looked like senators of ancient Rome. Closer to me, the pair of couches that Holmes and I generally occupied lay side-by-side.

At the moment, however, two silver-haired gentlemen, both about sixty-years-old and also wrapped in white, were casually stretched out on the red-damask cushions. The hair of one man was short and neatly coiffed; the hair of the other, as ragged as a bird's nest. This second gentleman sported shaggy eyebrows as well as a dark walrus moustache that covered the upper lip of a delicate mouth. In fact, his was a familiar face, one I believed I'd seen in countless photographs.

Their distance was some twenty-five feet from me and the fountain continued to gurgle, but I could still overhear not only most of their words but also the flat vowels of their American accents.

"Have you changed your opinion yet, Sam?" the clean-shaven man was asking his companion.

"No matter how much it's helped with my gout," the other said in a slow drawl, "I swore I'd never come back to one of these places—not after that Turkish bath in Constantinople. Why, I was nearly killed with all that rubbing and pounding. And I won't even dignify with a single word the mud they served as coffee." The more irritated he sounded, the higher climbed the pitch of his voice.

The other gentleman offered his companion a long cigar, struck a match, and leaned toward him to light his friend's cigar as well as his own. Almost immediately, the chamber filled with the rich scent of expensive tobacco.

"And *now*," the shorthaired gentleman asked, "what do you think of these baths?"

The man with the drawl nodded in thanks and then, with his eyes shut, took a long pull. "And *now*?" he repeated, opening his eyes and waving his cigar in the general direction of the entire room. "And *now*? Why, *this* hall of happiness, *this* chamber of comfort, *this* den of delight—*this* is another story. This *English* bath house is more like what a *Turkish* bath is supposed to be."

"As I told you," said his friend.

Both men lay back on the couches, sucked on their cigars, and smiled at what could only be the vagaries of life that had positioned them so opportunely.

After a few moments, the man with the unruly hair looked round once more. "Would you believe," he declared, "that except for all the changing of clothes and—I should hope—the protestations of my wife, I could move right in to this place? I swear, I can imagine leaving my suit at home and showing up here in my bathrobe and slippers. I swear, one day, that's just what I'm going to do!"

Need I hear more? The bold threat of walking barelegged down a London street and the niggling criticisms of an authentic Turkish bath made me all but certain of the man's identity.

One other fact helped solidify my opinion. By the turn of the century, London and its environs had become a mecca for American authors. Bret Harte lived at Lancaster Gate not three miles from where I was at that instant reclining. Harold Frederic resided alternately in Hammersmith and Croydon. Henry James, who'd occupied rooms in De Vere Gardens in 1887 when he'd come to Holmes regarding the Aspen Papers, had moved to Rye a few years previous. The recently deceased Stephen Crane had held court in a run-down manor house near Hastings, which I described in the adventure called *Sherlock Holmes and the Baron of Brede Place.*

Because of this American prominence and because, like so many other readers, I too had laughed my way through the exaggerations and complaints of foreign life in *The Innocents Abroad,* I felt quite comfortable in identifying the man I'd been overhearing. Even a reader like Sherlock Holmes, whose knowledge of literature I'd once labelled "nil", could have recognised that cigar-smoking, older American topped with a whirlwind of white hair. Lounging across the room that day at Nevill's Turkish Baths was none other than Samuel Langhorne Clemens.

The writer in me realized that the briefest of encounters with so talented an artist could offer much pleasure, and I vowed not to waste the moment. It was simply too great an opportunity to miss. And so I put down my pipe, eased my feet into my bath slippers and, girding the white sheet tightly round my body, hobbled across the tiled floor towards the two gentlemen in question.

* * *

Ah, sweet innocence! The singular person who might have advised me of the black cloud hovering above the pair that day had not accompanied me to Nevill's; and I, left to fend for myself, never realized the implications. Those first few steps of mine were but the start of a perilous journey, a meandering venture that would last many years, involve numerous innocents, and send one poor wretch to the gallows.

Later that evening, Sherlock Holmes would tell me he'd spent a relaxing afternoon listening to Wagner at Covent Garden.

Chapter Three

Prosperity is the best protector of principle.
--Mark Twain
"Pudd'nhead Wilson's
New Calendar"

Within moments, I was being scrutinized by sharp eyes of clearest blue, the upturned outer tips of the dark brows adding fierceness to the gaze. Yet no sooner did I announce my name than a broad smile radiated from the face before me.

"Sam Clemens," its owner proclaimed, vigorously shaking my hand as if we'd been acquainted for years. "I know who *you* are, sir," he astonished me by saying. "You're that doctor fella who writes about the detective, Sherlock Holmes. I *heard* that the two of you sometimes stop in here."

My cheeks flushed in response. "Unfortunately, today I'm here alone."

"I've read pretty much all your accounts," Clemens continued, the tufted eyebrows rising in a form of exclamatory punctuation. "Damn good stuff, if you don't mind my saying so."

"Of course, I don't mind," said I, blushing anew. "I appreciate your interest." A compliment from any writer is especially valued; a compliment from Samuel Clemens soars beyond the realm of one's dreams. "'Damn good stuff'," the man had actually said of my work.

Pleased as I was, I must still point out that neither was I so blinded by Clemens' compliment nor forgetful of my training from Holmes that I failed to note the curious reaction of Clemens' silver-haired companion. Originally relaxed and gazing into space, he shifted his cold, grey eyes in my direction without actually turning his head, a crafty, nervous move—or so it seemed to me. What's more, unless I was very much mistaken, this new demeanour appeared at exactly the instant the famed writer had mentioned the word "detective".

Clemens interrupted my contemplations by indicating the man about whom I was just then thinking. "This gentleman is Senator J. Neil Gibson—formerly of Nevada and California. Don't hold his origins against him though; he's been living here in England for the past five years. He's got a manor house in Hampshire called 'Thor Place'. You may have heard of him referred to as 'The Gold King'. Even so, *I* still call him 'Jed', the name he went by out West. *He* prefers 'Senator'—though that clearly identifies him as a member of the United States Congress." Here Clemens paused to draw on his cigar. His timing might have been rehearsed. "The United States Congress," he mused, eyebrows shooting up, "the only native criminal class we Americans have to boast of."

In spite of Clemens' humour, his strong-jawed friend displayed no smile; perhaps he'd heard the joke before. He simply nodded curtly in my direction and pointed his cigar at me to stress his words: "*Former* member."

I recognized neither Gibson's name nor his sobriquet, and I couldn't be sure whether the Senator was jesting with a poker face or seriously emphasizing a point. It all seemed to matter very little, however, for in the next instant he turned his cold eyes away, obviously less interested in me than was his companion.

Clemens waved his cigar in the general direction of some empty chairs set against a nearby wall. "Pull up a seat, why don't you, Doctor."

Relishing the opportunity to spend some time with so accomplished a writer, I thanked him profusely and, as gracefully as my sheet would allow, carried one of the chairs over to where the two men reclined

Clemens sucked noisily at his cigar as I lowered myself onto the cushion.

"Like I was saying," he went on, "I follow your stories about Sherlock Holmes pretty regularly. I reckon you could call my interest 'professional'."

"Professional"?

"You may not be aware of it, Doctor, but I too have devoted a bit of time to writing detective stories. 'Course, unlike yours, mine are fiction."

"I didn't know," I confessed, sensing my limitations in the realm of American letters. "I'm sure they're of the highest quality," I added lamely. "Like all your others. Everyone in England loves those travel books—not to mention *Tom Sawyer* and *Huckleberry Finn*."

"*You*, sir," said Clemens, pointing his cigar at me, "have excellent taste in literature. Oh, I know that most people consider me some sort of humourist, and I suppose I am. But I really *have* written a few mystery yarns—even if they do tend towards the burlesque." He offered a soft chuckle, all the while continuing to fix me with his blue eyes. Probing my brain for ideas about fictional detective stories might not be beyond his thinking.

For his part, Senator Gibson pulled on his cigar. Clearly, he'd had enough of this literary conversation.

"In fact," Clemens went on undeterred, "I invented a 'tec of my own—though he's no Sherlock Holmes. Simon Wheeler, I call him—modelled after the late Allan Pinkerton and some of his boys. I even *appropriated*—Pinkerton called it 'stealing'—his insignia, the staring eye, and the motto, "We Never Sleep". And why shouldn't I use them, I'd like to know? My detective's as clever as Pinkerton's—maybe even *more* clever."

On that score, I fancied Clemens must have been right. I'd always regarded Pinkerton's memoirs about his American detective agency as too self-congratulatory.

"Just like the 'Pinks'," continued Clemens, "Simon Wheeler wears disguises, eaves-drops, and holes up in secret hiding places. I may be biased, of course; but as his creator, I think he does some pretty intelligent investigating. 'Course, no one else seems to think so. Why, I even wrote a play about him though the damn thing went bust." By way of illustration, Sam Clemens took a pull on his cigar and blew a white cloud into the air in the general direction of the dome. "Up in smoke," he added—in case I missed the point.

I watched the wispy tendrils curl upward whilst I contemplated Clemens as a crime writer. *Tom Sawyer* contained a murder, after all; and Huckleberry Finn staged his own death. It took no great imagination to visualize the man as a writer of mystery stories.

My thoughts were cut short, however, as the Senator cleared his throat with obvious determination. Apparently, he was ready to leave. Normally, I would have responded to the hint; normally, I wouldn't have wanted to overstay my welcome. But how often does one get the opportunity to converse with a writer of Samuel Clemens' stature?

"You might also be interested to know, Dr. Watson," continued Clemens, oblivious to his friend's desire, "that in *Tom*

Sawyer, Detective, one of my more recent mystery tales, Huck Finn is the narrator."

"Interesting."

My reaction must not have been enthusiastic enough; for Clemens immediately added, "Don't you see, Doctor? Huck played *Dr. Watson* to Tom Sawyer's Sherlock Holmes!"

"Ah," said I, bowing my head. "I'm duly honoured."

I was clearly in the man's good graces, and I couldn't see allowing Clemens' friend, however uncomfortable or bored he might be, to break up our meeting just yet. A few more questions, I surmised, might extend our time together. It should require but the slightest of promptings, I reasoned, to encourage a world-famous raconteur like Samuel Clemens to commence a story.

"How did you two gentlemen meet?" I dared to ask.

Clemens didn't disappoint me—though Gibson seemed perturbed. The former Senator knitted his brow. Clemens, obviously readying himself to deliver some sort of intricate monologue, extracted the cigar from his mouth and leaned back into the deep cushion. He might as well have been performing on a stage.

"In 1861," the writer said, picking at some stray bits of tobacco left on his tongue, "I joined my brother Orion on a trip out West. Orion had been appointed the secretary to the governor of the Nevada Territory; and since my work as a riverboat pilot on the Mississippi had dried up with the start of our Civil War, I decided to go along with him. I guess you could say I was sort of a secretary *to* the secretary."

He grinned for an instant, pleased at his turn of phrase—or, perhaps, pleased in anticipation of the memory he was about to report. "Don't think I wasn't a patriot. I wasn't avoiding my military obligation. Originally, just after the War had commenced,

I joined a Confederate brigade. 'The Marion Rangers' we called ourselves—named after the Missouri county I used to live in. Where Hannibal was. 'Course, I did retire a short time later—I got tired of all the retreating."

"'A *short* time later'?" the Senator snorted. "You make it sound drawn out—like it could have been months or maybe even a year before you pulled out. As I heard tell, Sam, it was more like two weeks. Now can we—"

I was sure that Gibson was going to insist that they leave, but Clemens ignored the interruption and went right on. "Word got to us that the Union Army was coming to Marion County to track down irregulars like ourselves. That's when I decided to go west with Orion. Seemed a lot safer than being a soldier." Clemens inhaled some more smoke—it was a way he had of prolonging the suspense. He waited an additional moment, blew out another white cloud, and only then added the *coup de grâce*: "You know that it was just four years after I quit the Rangers that the Confederacy fell."

Even Gibson smiled.

"One can only wonder, Mr. Clemens," said I, going along with his joke, "what would have happened had you remained. The United States might be two separate countries today."

"It might at that," he said. "It might indeed be two separate countries today, but I doubt it." He shot a quick glance at his friend; perhaps Clemens was anticipating an argument. When he got none, he offered, "By the way, Doctor, you can call me 'Sam'. Most of my friends do anyhow."

But 'Sam' wasn't the name I associated with this literary figure.

"Surely," I countered, "you must sometimes call yourself 'Mark Twain'."

"That's true enough," said he.

"Especially," added his friend, "in greeting bartenders when he wants them to *mark* a couple of drinks."

Clemens shook his head. "Those days are long gone, Jed."

"Sorry," said the Senator. "I almost forgot your cover story—that on the river, 'Mark Twain' means 'safe passage'."

Clemens ignored Gibson's comment and resumed his tale. "I had high hopes when I got to Nevada. But it didn't take me long to see that there wasn't any money in assisting my brother. That's when I figured I'd join the crowd and take up silver mining. What with the silver just lying around for the taking—or so I thought."

Senator Gibson sighed heavily. No doubt he'd heard the story before.

"I headed for Virginia City out in the Washoe—that's the Indian name for the Nevada territory—and then on to Esmeralda County."

"So I've read."

"In *Roughing It*," the writer confirmed. "But if I may be allowed to quote Dr. Watson's *Doppelgänger*, my own Huckleberry Finn, 'Mr. Mark Twain, he told the truth—*mainly*'."

The humour was in the pause before that final word. Never have I heard anyone handle silence more effectively.

"Well," said Clemens, "I went bust out *there* too. Came close a couple times; but in the end, it was all just hard work with nothing much to show. So I changed direction again and took a job with the *Territorial Enterprise*, a local newspaper in Virginia City. I did all right with the *Enterprise*, but eventually I got bored at that outfit as well. That was when I left Esmeralda and headed for San Francisco. I got a writing job in the city—with the *Morning Call*, where I met a lot of literary types. Writers you wouldn't have heard of back then—fellas like Joaquin Miller and

Bret Harte."

Gibson slowly shook his head at the mention of their names.

"I hadn't heard of them 'back then'," said I, politely omitting the fact that I wasn't much more than a child at the time. "Nor have I read either one. But I do know that Miller visited London years ago, and I believe that Bret Harte's been living here for quite some time."

"Free-loading's more like it," Sam Clemens muttered half to himself, "posing like some English lord though he's got no money."

Now that he'd mentioned it, I did recall some unflattering tales related to Bret Harte. If memory served, people said he was living with a wealthy widow at Lancaster Gate, having left his wife of thirty years back in America to fend for herself.

"Sam," prodded Gibson, "I'm sure that Dr. Watson isn't interested in your tittle-tattle about other writers."

But I *was*, of course—even though I remained completely unaware of the sinister implications swirling about me in the guise of gossip. On that afternoon I was just happy to listen to Clemens roll on like a runaway railway carriage:

"Now Joaquin Miller was just the opposite of Bret Hart. Oh, like lots of Americans over here, Miller was a poseur; but his guise was more cowboy than literary man. It must have been close to thirty years ago, but I can still see him with his shoulder-long hair and thick beard prancing around in buckskin, leather boots, bandana, and slouch hat. Sometimes he'd even wear a red sash and stick a huge knife in his belt. Why, he used to put on his chaps and spurs and gallop on horseback right through Hyde Park. He'd been a rider for the Pony Express, you know."

"My word," I said. I did recall something about Miller's

western persona, but his equestrian pursuits were another matter.

"Yes sir," Clemens smiled behind a cloud of smoke, "he was quite the performer was old Joaquin."

Gibson rolled his eyes. Poor fellow. Maybe he was in such a hurry to leave so he could avoid hearing the familiar stories all over again.

"I remember a dinner Miller and I both attended," continued Clemens. "It was at the Garrick Club here in London back in the early 70's. We were served some kind of fish, and damned if Joaquin didn't pick the thing up by its tale and swallow it whole."

"My word," said I again.

"We were guests of your author, Anthony Trollope, you see. But you should have heard him and Miller go at it—Trollope, with his King's English; Miller, with his Western slang. They talked constantly—and usually at the same time. Miller billed himself the 'Poet of the Sierras', but his poetry was good enough to get him re-christened here as the 'Frontier Poet of Mayfair'. I recall one poem in particular he wrote about Columbus—if you could read his scrawl. Miller said an Indian arrow had struck him in the right wrist some years before, and it slowed up his writing."

"*Red* Indians? They're always a favourite. It's no wonder we English loved him."

"You can bank on it," Clemens winked. "Old Joaquin surely did—'bank on it', I mean. He knew how to please an audience. I actually learned quite a bit from Miller's showmanship. Let's not forget that I had my own title back then: 'The Wild Humourist of the Western Slope'. Don't get me wrong. I didn't walk around in cowboy togs like old Joaquin, though I was known to sport a string tie at my lectures in those days—and sometimes I even wore an oversized sealskin hat and coat."

"But you told no Indian stories," said I.

"None to speak of. At least none like Miller's. Depending on whose history you want to believe, he either fought with—or against—the Modocs. They're a tribe in northern California." Here Clemens paused, his reflections taking a more serious turn. "We gave our daughter Suzy the nickname 'Modoc' because she was so headstrong a child. She died almost four years ago. She was twenty-four. But when she was little—why, she learned to swear and stand up at almost the same time."

"Surely there must have been people who resented Miller," said I, "people who found him too full of American-style self-promotion. You yourself said that Bret Harte was just the opposite. *He* must have regarded Miller's fame as low-class notoriety."

The mention of Bret Harte drained the sea of nostalgia in which Sam Clemens had immersed himself. He now seemed ready to pounce. "Why, Bret Harte—"

But then he just waved his hand in the air—as if to be rid of the topic, as if Bret Harte wasn't worth the effort that belittling him required. "Let's just say that I once compared the man to an oyster. Later," Clemens deadpanned. "I realized I'd have to apologize to the oyster."

Apparently, Sam Clemens wasn't the only one to be bothered by Bret Harte. The mention of Harte's name seemed to disturb Gibson as well. The Senator had said nothing during the discussion of Joaquin Miller, but he nervously began to rearrange the sheet in which he was wrapped as soon as Clemens started insulting Bret Harte. At the same time, the furrows in Gibson's brow grew deeper, and his jaw appeared more firmly set.

Clemens also noted Gibson's reaction. "Old Jed, here," said

the writer, "couldn't stomach Harte's flim-flam either."

Suddenly, Senator Gibson stood up. He was a tall man of powerful build. "I think it's high time for us to be leaving."

Clemens, however, waved him down.

I'm sure the Gold King was unused to taking orders, but he nonetheless sank back onto the red-damask couch.

"I already told you," said Clemens, "that this place is good for my gout."

I fancied that his desire to remain had less to do with his health than with the opportunity to continue speaking.

"Now where was I?" Clemens asked as if the *contretemps* between him and Gibson had never occurred. "Seems to me I was telling you about San Francisco."

"Right," said I as Gibson seethed.

"Well," Clemens began again, "after a while, I got into a mite of trouble with some of the local authorities. Seems that they didn't appreciate what I was writing about them and wanted to force me into some new direction. That's when I decided that maybe I needed another change of scenery. It didn't help that my old friend Steve Gillis had been arrested there for fighting." Clemens turned to Gibson. "You remember Steve Gillis, don't you, Jed—my so-called enforcer?"

The Senator's jaw slackened, relaxing at the memory. "'The Pepper Pot'? Oh, I remember Steve all right. Less than five feet tall and under a hundred pounds. But he was quite the brawler, especially with that sharp right cross." Cigar in hand, Gibson made a punching motion. "We met in San Francisco back in the good old days—before *you* ever got there, Sam—and we immediately took to each other. Steve Gillis and I closed down a few bars together, I can tell you that."

"Maybe you did," said Clemens, "and maybe you two were

tight as thunder and lightning. All I know is that we were roommates for a time, and *I* was the one he called to post his bail when he got arrested, and *I* was the one who got stuck with the bill when he ignored my bond and took off. He made for that rundown cabin his older brother Jim owned up in the Sierra foothills. About a hundred miles east of San Francisco. Turned out though, that all things considered—financially, not to mention politically—it made sense for *me* to leave San Francisco just then too. So I ended up joining him."

Senator Gibson snorted in response, and Sam Clemens took the opportunity to savour his cigar.

A few puffs later, Clemens continued the story. "It was late 1864, and Steve and I settled in for a sort of vacation out there in the wilderness. Jim's place stood on a low rise in Calaveras County called Jackass Hill. Remember, Jed? It was mighty beautiful country out there in the mountains. One ridge climbing up after another, all of them covered with fir trees as far as you could see. In the winter, those ridges looked like soft blankets of white wool piled up to the sky."

"I remember the landscape all right," said the Senator. "I'm—I'm not so clear on the cabin."

"I'm surprised, Jed—that's where you and I met—to answer Dr. Watson's question."

To be honest, I'd forgot I'd asked the question. But Gibson shrugged, and Clemens stared at his friend for a few moments.

"Don't you recall? It had this one large room with a packed-dirt floor and a fireplace below a high mantel. There were so many pieces of furniture in the place that I swear a body could get lost behind them. You really don't remember?"

"No, I don't," Gibson said defiantly.

"No matter. The cabin burned down a few years ago. But,

you know, I always thought that 'Jackass Hill' was a good name for the place. It got its title from the donkeys that carried supplies in pack trains up to the mining camps. When gold was in season, some two hundred burros might be tethered around the cabin. Shoot, they made enough racket to raise the dead; it was like they owned the whole mountainside. As a consequence, I never quarrelled with the name, especially because it was called 'Jackass Hill' before *I* ever got there. It was a good moniker, all right; in fact, you could make a pile of money using it to rename the earth."

Gibson surprised me by laughing at Clemens' little joke. The Senator had been staring off into space, and I thought he'd once again lost interest in the writer's rambling tale. But I was wrong. His laugh was a queer sort though: his eyes didn't participate. In retrospect, I suppose that I shouldn't have been surprised that he was listening. A man like J. Neil Gibson didn't become one of the world's great gold magnates by ignoring what was going on round him.

"The Gillis cabin," continued Clemens, "had a sort of open-door policy. Everybody knew it. All sorts of people, including writers—*especially* writers—would go there. Why, they'd park themselves on these wooden barrels that pretended to be chairs and partake from this rickety old table just loaded with books waiting to be read: Byron, Shakespeare, Dickens. I do believe old Joaquin passed through; I know Bret Harte did because the two of us went up to the cabin together once—when we are on good terms—and he told me he'd been there before. Fellas would stay a couple of days or even a week or two—talk some, read some, eat a bit, and drink a lot. You remember that much, don't you, Jed?"

The Senator shrugged.

"Once I stayed three months—eighty-eight days to be exact. During the wet winter of '64 and '65. Why, it was so cold that winter you had to suck on ice to keep yourself warm. It was sometime around then that Jim Gillis stood up in front of their big fireplace and told me the story of that jumping frog. Who could have known back in those days that a talented frog would be the mother lode for me?"

Attentive readers with even the most rudimentary knowledge of Clemens' career knew that the publication of his story about a frog-jumping contest in Calaveras County had gained him his initial entry into the world of *belles-lettres* and eventually fame and fortune.

"Now that I recall, Jed," Clemens went on, "that same winter was the time *we* first met. Remember?" Clemens pointed his cigar at Gibson. "I'd been there awhile already. Oh, sometimes I'd ride off to Angels Camp to look for gold—it was about ten miles north of Jackass Hill—but eventually I'd come back to the cabin. One of those times, you were stopping there. You said you'd just missed out on the Comstock Lode. And I said, '—you and a couple thousand other fellas, including me.' You said you'd just finished law school and wanted to try some prospecting out in the Washoe before you hung up your law shingle."

Gibson nodded passively.

"In fact, I do believe I saw you there at least one other time—maybe it was when I went up there with Bret Harte."

The Senator struggled with his sheet again. "Yes," he finally said, "I guess I stayed there on a few occasions. I must have forgotten."

At first, he couldn't remember the cabin; now he was saying he'd been there more than once.

"Bret Harte," muttered the Senator. "For all your complaining about the man, Sam, *you're* the one who introduced me to him."

Now it was Sam Clemens' chance to offer a snort. "Bret Harte," he muttered, biting down on the cigar. Suddenly, he cried out, "I remember now! That was the day some stranger told the story about the baby raised by a pack of miners."

Gibson nodded "Steve Gillis had invited me back," the Senator explained slowly. It seemed important for him to get the facts right. Then, for only an instant, he stopped talking, and his eyes narrowed. Were I less charitable, I might describe his expression as cruel.

"I remember," said Clemens again. "You were a sight—I scarcely recognized you. Your hair was long and stringy; your beard was all grown out. And you hung around in the darkness best I can remember. You didn't look much like a lawyer, I can tell you that."

Gibson shook his head, eyes downcast.

"Bret Harte said the same when I introduced him to you and told him you'd just recently finished law school."

Now both of them sat there pondering the past.

Not for long, however. Clemens grumbled Harte's name again, and his cheeks began to flush. The mere thought of Bret Harte still seemed to annoy him.

"He didn't pay his debts!" Clemens erupted. "And he wore that infernal red tie. It looked like a flash of flame under his chin— or, or—better yet—like a Brazilian butterfly. In the early days I liked Bret Harte—then I got over it. Why, just look at what the rapscallion did after hearing that story up in the cabin. Do you know Bret Harte's 'The Luck of Roaring Camp', Doctor?"

I admitted that I did not. At the mention of the title, Senator Gibson fidgeted some more.

"You remember, Jed. That was the first time we heard the tale about the miners raising a baby. There was this fella at the cabin who offered up the true facts. What was his name? It had a funny ring to it."

"I don't recall," said Gibson.

But that didn't stop Sam Clemens—not when bringing up the meeting in the cabin allowed him to resume his rant against Bret Harte.

"The difference between Harte and me is that *I* never used that story. We both promised that fella we wouldn't—gave our word on it. Why, the difference between Bret Harte's word and this cigar is that it takes a passel of time for the cigar to go up in smoke. Harte said he wouldn't write the story, but he still went off and did it. Published it *himself*. Sure, it might be the best thing he's ever written—which isn't saying much—but it was wrong to make public what had happened when he said he wouldn't. Plain wrong! And all that tripe about the baby? Why, it was his attempt to sound like Dickens—though he's just a pathetic imitation. Bret Harte drills for tears the way those mechanical rigs drill for oil."

"Perhaps," I dared to say, "you're being too critical."

Sam Clemens' face grew even more florid. "Dr. Watson," he charged, "Bret Harte is the most contemptible little blatherskite that ever occupied the planet!"

The damning words echoed round the cavernous dome of the drying-room.

Hoping to calm Clemens' anger, I turned to the Senator. "You were starting to tell us about *your* trip to the cabin, Senator—when Steve Gillis invited you back up there." I really *was* curious; the pugnacious Gillis seemed like the kind of American we English thought them all to be.

The Senator frowned. I'd offered my suggestion in hopes of hearing more about Jackass Hill and the colourful Gillises; but this time round, Gibson took the opportunity to turn the

30

conversation away from the infamous cabin.

"Once I determined that there wasn't any gold left to find in the Sierras," said he, "I decided to clear out. Though I hadn't made much in the Washoe before then, I'd gained enough money from working a small silver vein to move on. It was the early fifties, and I ended up staking myself to a gold mine near Sacramento. People warned me that most all the gold had been extracted from the general vicinity, and I guess it *had* been around Sutter's Mill. But I reckon God or luck or both were on my side. I still had the fever, and it wasn't long before I'd made enough money from my latest stake to pay for a trip to Brazil. I'd heard there was still gold to be found down there. Some old-timers told me to head for the town of Ouro Preto in an area known as the Minas Gerais; and, sure enough, not long after I got there, I struck it rich in the mountains of Serra do Espinhaço."

"How ironical," I observed. "The American known as 'The Gold King' actually made his fortune in Brazil."

"Gold is gold wherever you find it," Gibson philosophized.

"But it wasn't just *gold* he found," said Clemens, exhaling yet another cloud of smoke. "He discovered his beautiful wife, Maria Pinto, down there as well."

"Not during my mining days, however," the Senator said, squirming once more. "By the time I met Maria, I was already a rich man."

Clemens raised his shaggy eyebrows. "By then, Jed had begun putting on airs. He ran around San Francisco with millionaires like Aloysius Doran. You remember him, Doctor? The prospector who struck it rich working a claim in McQuire's camp near the Rockies? A few years back, you wrote about his daughter Hatty in 'The Noble Bachelor'."

"Indeed, I do," said I. Who wouldn't remember the curious

31

affair of a wedding gone horribly wrong? The bride had disappeared during the breakfast that immediately followed the ceremony.

"It was living among all those rich folks," Sam Clemens went on, "that got my friend here to change his name. Well, he gave up the 'Jed' anyway—started calling himself 'J. Neil'."

Doubtlessly preferring a switch in subject to being skewered by Sam Clemens, the Senator resumed talking about his wife: "I wanted to see the rain forests and was traveling from my gold mines across the Brazilian countryside. I met Maria in Manaos."

"Maria's a *younger* woman," explained Clemens with a lascivious wink. "Old J. Neil here has always liked 'em young. And they like *him*—especially when he has his moneybags on. Course, *now* things are different. They have two children."

"And a governess to care for them," Gibson added, smiling wistfully.

"I ran into Jed a few years ago in New York, and we resumed our friendship. Can't say that he laughs a lot anymore, but we have similar memories of our time out West. And neither of us can abide Bret Harte. Maybe that's why we're friends. We never did like the way he looked at our wives. Reminds me of myself in the Sandwich Islands—but I reckon that's another story . . . ."

The Senator stared off again. He might have been savouring memories of those earlier days, and yet his gaze remained stone-cold.

Sam Clemens contemplated his cigar. "Doctor," said he, "do you know what would really cap off this conversation?"

Perfectly content, I shook my head, wondering what might come next.

"Well, sir, let me tell you. I'd surely appreciate it if you could arrange a meeting for me with Sherlock Holmes."

Senator Gibson put up a cautioning hand. "Now, Sam," he said, "I don't think—"

"No, Jed, I mean it. I'd love to talk detectin' with Sherlock Holmes. I've already confessed to you that most of my early mystery tales were of a comical nature. But in the last few years I've gotten more serious, and I'd like his opinion on some matters that concern me."

Along with a plume of smoke, Gibson let out a sigh of frustration.

"My family and I are living in Dollis Hill House over at Kilburn until the end of September," Clemens said. "It's a beautiful place. You think you're out in the country, but it's just seventeen minutes to Baker Street."

"Exactly seventeen?" I chortled. "You seem mighty certain. Did you actually clock the journey?"

"I did, in fact, Doctor. On the Metropolitan line. There's a photographer I like at No. 42 Baker Street. Fella named Histed. I consulted my pocket watch so that when I wrote to my old friend Joe Twichell back in the States, I could be precise: 'By rail,' I told him, 'we can be in the heart of London, in Baker Street, in seventeen minutes'." With another wink, he added, "'By a smart train, in five'."

I laughed accordingly; the Senator was not even smiling.

As we all prepared to depart, I said to Clemens, "I'll see what I can do about arranging that meeting for you with Sherlock Holmes."

* * *

Alas, such a meeting never took place—at least, not in the manner that Clemens or I had fancied.

I left Nevill's enveloped in giddiness, no longer bothered by the nip in the air that had prompted my visit to the baths in the first place. All the way home, I continued to relish my experience with one of the great celebrities of our era. John Watson had just spent a glorious hour in the company of Samuel Langhorne Clemens! What's more, John Watson actually had his writings praised by the man! And once I arranged the additional visit with Holmes, there would be yet another chance to converse with him.

But Holmes' so-called "detectin'" and my immediate surgery consumed much of our time during the next few months, and neither my friend nor I seemed able to find the opportunity. As is often the case when the glow of enthusiasm dims, in spite of all the excitement the meeting at Nevill's had engendered, my offer to bring the two great men together had slipped my mind.

The story does not end there, however. If it had, the world might have been a happier place. In early October, just days before he was to sail for America, Sam Clemens made another appearance at 221B, albeit not for anything having to do with crime writing—indeed, not for anything having to do with *fictional* detecting at all. On the contrary, along with his friend Senator Gibson, Sam Clemens came to consult with Sherlock Holmes about the unsatisfying resolution of an all-too-real murder—a murder that, unbeknownst to me at the time, had occurred on a bridge at the Senator's home in Hampshire a few weeks before.

Chapter Four

I believe I have no prejudices whatsoever. All I need to know is that a man is a member of the human race. That's bad enough for me.
--Mark Twain
Notebooks

"Do you recall Senator J. Neil Gibson?" Sherlock Holmes asked as I was finishing my kedgeree and coffee. It was a windy Thursday morning, the fourth of October to be precise, some four months after my visit to Nevill's. Nestled in front of a crackling fire, Holmes had evidently concluded his breakfast well before I began my trek down the stairs.

In truth, I'd been enjoying the warmth of my bed. There was a decided wail from the wind outside, punctuated by the clanging of a metal dustbin as it bounced somewhere down Baker Street. Tree branches scratched frantically against a casement window; and shadows, accompanied by the rustle of the *débris* from the single large plane tree in the yard behind our building, danced across the curtains.

By the time I sat down to eat, Holmes was hard at work, assiduously pasting newspaper cuttings onto the brown pages of one of his scrapbooks. In such a manner, he maintained his personal file of various crimes, which he would frequently review. He placed great faith in the concept that specific patterns of criminal behaviour in a past case might help him identify the perpetrator within a current investigation.

"I asked," said Holmes, "if you recall Senator J. Neil Gibson?"

"Sorry," said I, coming to terms with being awake. "Of course, I remember him. He's the gentleman I met at Nevill's last summer when you were at the opera." The mention of Nevill's evoked a pinch of guilt. "It was the day I introduced myself to Samuel Clemens—the day I promised to invite him here, but never did."

"Quite so," said Holmes distractedly. "But it is Senator Gibson I'm talking about."

I shrugged my shoulders. "Oh, I know—the man is considered a financial titan. But to me, Holmes, he was simply the person who happened to be seated along side Samuel L. Clemens."

In silence, I finished a final bite of egg, wondering why he'd enquired of Gibson. Holmes continued to fiddle with his cuttings.

"Coffee?" I asked, holding up the silver pot.

He came to the table, seated himself, and held out his cup. "With such limited interest in the Senator, Watson," said he whilst I began dispensing the brew, "I take it that you didn't read of the violent murder of his wife a fortnight past."

I immediately stopped pouring. "Murder, Holmes? I've heard nothing of the matter."

Holmes nodded at the open scrapbooks on his cluttered desk. "I've been putting the cuttings into my files, but—"

And you didn't think to inform me?" From the street, a howl of wind mocked my displeasure.

"To what end?" he asked, still holding out the cup. "You encountered the Senator in passing. He was nothing to you. You just told me as much. To discuss the death of his wife under such circumstances would be the most idle form of gossip."

With a sigh of exasperation, I finished pouring his coffee. Unlike Holmes, I wasn't afraid to admit that I often found myself amused by empty chatter, especially when it concerned people I actually knew. Death, of course, altered the nature of the conversation.

"Tell me of this murder, Holmes," said I as I set down the coffee pot. "At Nevill's, Gibson did make passing reference to his wife. If I recall correctly, the unfortunate woman's name was Maria Pinto, and she was from Brazil."

"Yes, Watson," said Holmes, adding a splash of milk to the steaming brew, "you're quite right. But more to the point, Senator Gibson sent me a letter from Claridge's yesterday. In it, he asked for an appointment this morning at 11:00. He made no mention of the reason for the meeting, but one can offer an educated guess."

"Surely, it must be related to the murder of his wife."

"Aye, Watson," he said, holding up his forefinger, "and there's the rub. According to the newspaper accounts, the Gibsons' governess, a Miss Grace Dunbar, has already been apprehended. Miss Dunbar's guilt seems to be what the Americans call an 'open-and-shut' case. The proceedings before two courts—the police court and the coroner's—have already resulted in her being detained for the next Assizes."

"If two courts agree, then this Miss Dunbar must certainly be guilty."

"Presumably, Watson," said he, returning to his coffee. "But allow me to give you the most significant of the details regarding the case. That way, if the murder of Maria Gibson does turn out to be the subject of our meeting, you will be familiar with the salient features."

I drank my coffee slowly, listening to Holmes recount the facts he'd gleaned from the various newspaper stories—all of which I accurately presented in my previously-published account of the tragedy called "The Problem of Thor Bridge": At 11:00 at night some two weeks earlier, the body of Senator Gibson's wife had been found by the gamekeeper at the mouth of Thor Bridge about half a mile from the Senator's manor house in Hampshire. Still dressed in the gown she'd worn to dinner, Mrs. Gibson had been shot in the head, the bullet entering her skull just behind the right temple. Her left hand was clutching a small, rumpled paper upon which was written in the handwriting of the governess: "I will be at Thor Bridge at nine o'clock." The note was signed "G. Dunbar".

Other than the bullet wound, there were no marks on the body and no sign of a struggle. Powder burns indicated that the gun had been fired at close range. The note led investigators to Miss Dunbar's room where, on the floor of her wardrobe, a revolver with one chamber emptied was discovered. The calibre of the gun matched that of the fatal bullet, and a passing pedestrian claimed to have seen the governess at the bridge near the time of the shooting. The evidence was sufficient to have Miss Dunbar remanded to the Assizes at Winchester to await trial for murder.

I shrugged. "The police found the murder weapon in her wardrobe, you say? As much as I hate to see a member of the fairer sex accused of so heinous a crime, the case against the woman seems convincing. What can Senator Gibson expect you to do?"

"My thoughts exactly, Watson. One can only surmise that the Senator is looking for straws to grasp. But unless I'm very much mistaken, we shall soon get the answer to your question."

Holmes was reacting to the tattoo of a pair of footsteps rapidly approaching our door. I recognized one set as belonging to the pageboy Billy; the other, I presumed, to Senator Gibson. It was still a few minutes before the scheduled meeting time, but I was not surprised to hear the page knocking for admittance to announce the man's early arrival.

Holmes and I reached for our jackets, and then I answered the door. Preceded by a gust of cold air that had invaded the premises when he'd opened the front door downstairs, the boy in buttons stepped inside our rooms and adjusted the tunic of his burgundy livery. Much to our surprise, however, after he'd cleared his throat, it was not the name of Senator Gibson he voiced.

"Mr. Marlow Bates," Billy trumpeted, only to be unceremoniously shoved aside by the short, pasty-faced man in question.

"See here!" I exploded at the newcomer, rising to my feet, arms outstretched, to offer the lad some assistance.

Billy simply straightened his uniform. An angry blast of wind rattled the windows behind us, but Billy nodded at Holmes and me and padded off down the stairs as if he hadn't noticed the rudeness to which he'd been subjected.

I, however, demanded an explanation. "What is the meaning of this invasion?"

"I'm—I'm sorry," the man said nervously, his accent American, "but I'm pressed for time." A small, pale fellow with wild, thinning hair, he appeared to be in his late thirties. Clad as he was in a brown-tweed suit, a black wool muffler, and high riding boots, I should have taken him for an English country gentleman had I not heard his flattened drawl or witnessed his discourteous entrance. In spite of his professed need for haste, he paused to gain composure, taking deep breaths and patting down his dishevelled hair.

I was the closer to him, and he addressed me first. "As you just heard, Mr. Holmes, my name is Marlow Bates, and I know you're meeting with Senator Gibson at eleven. I intend to speak my peace before he gets here."

"I'm Dr. John Watson." Indicating my friend, I said, "*This* is Mr. Sherlock Holmes."

He looked back and forth at the two of us, uncertainty flashing in his wild eyes.

"You're quite right, Mr. Bates," replied Holmes calmly. "I am indeed meeting with Senator Gibson at 11:00. But how you know that and why you are here I can only surmise. From your accent and your boots I perceive that you work on his estate, but—"

"He'll be here any minute," Bates interrupted. "I—I don't have time to listen to your feats of deduction, however acclaimed they may be."

I hadn't the foggiest notion what this ill-mannered man desired to say, but it seemed quite obvious that he didn't want the Senator to know he'd spoken to us.

"I'm the manager of Senator Gibson's property in Hampshire," the fellow said quickly. "Although, not for much longer. I'm planning to give him notice, you see. I can't work for that villain anymore. But I had to warn you, Mr. Holmes. That's why I've come—to tell you not to let his forked tongue fool you. He's a devil; make no mistake.

"He has some sort of twisted infatuation with Grace Dunbar, his children's governess, who, as I'm sure you know, has been remanded to the Assizes for killing Mrs. Gibson. Now, for his own selfish reasons, he wants her set free. She's quite beautiful, you see; and he wants her for himself. Parasite that she is, she wormed her way into his life through his children. And while you might turn a blind eye to the torment she has caused at Thor Place, you cannot ignore the role of that scheming bitch in Maria Gibson's cold-blooded murder."

"See here," said I, "whether you're in a hurry or not, I won't tolerate a woman's being spoken of so venomously—even if she *has* been incarcerated for murder."

Bates' eyes narrowed, as he appeared to be taking my measure. "Sounds like she's fooled you too, Doctor," said he, "and you haven't even met her." He was perspiring freely now and, producing a white handkerchief, proceeded to mop his pale brow.

"In spite of your epithets, Mr. Bates," countered Holmes, "you have told us nothing new."

"Don't you see?" the man cried. "Gibson's coming here to convince you to save his wife's murderer. The only way Grace Dunbar could get her hands on Gibson's money was by eliminating his wife. And now the stupid fool's trying to free her." He paused to catch his breath again. With his eyes wide open and trained on Holmes, he exclaimed, "I must run. He'll be here any minute. But I'm telling you, Mr Holmes: he's going to ask for your help in getting his wife's killer out of gaol."

Holmes arched his eyebrows at Bates' entreaty, but said nothing.

"I know your reputation," the man went on. "People say you do what's right and proper. I know you'll see through his lies. Just promise me you won't tell him I've come to see you. I've only done so because—in the name of Maria Gibson—I want to see justice prevail."

Leaving those noble words to hang in the air, Mr. Bates made an abrupt about-face, opened our door, and checked the stairwell. Finding the pathway clear, he dashed out, bounding down the steps two at a time.

"I say, Holmes! What do you make of that?"

There was no opportunity for an answer, however, since almost immediately the quick tread of Billy's feet on the stairs could be heard once again. Bates had been lucky to get out as quickly as he had, for certainly on *this* occasion Billy must now be followed by Senator Gibson.

And yet the footfalls trailing Billy's were too heavy and numerous for just a single caller. I might not have the deductive powers of my friend, but I could well distinguish the tread of multiple boots on a carpeted staircase that I myself climbed every day.

I opened the door to another gust of wind followed by Billy.

"Senator Gibson and Mr. Clemens," the lad announced.

We had expected the Senator; Sam Clemens was a surprise. Holmes and I had only a moment to exchange raised eyebrows before the two men, wrapped in dark overcoats and carrying short top hats, entered our sitting room.

Judging from Billy's especially erect posture, it appeared that presenting someone with the title of "Senator" greatly inflated the youth's sense of importance. He might have reacted similarly to announcing "Mark Twain", but I seriously doubted that the page knew who "Samuel Clemens" was. Still, I was pleased to watch him pause an extra moment to study more closely the visitor with the wild hair and the walrus moustache. I fancy that even a lad of Billy's young age must have sensed greatness in the slightly-stooped figure before him.

The boy helped the men remove their coats, and then he exited the room. As we all listened to him descending the stairs, I realized I had never seen the two visitors in their street clothes before. In our previous encounter, we had all three been enveloped in the togas of Nevill's bathhouse. Now I could appreciate the elegant figure the Senator presented in his pinstriped, navy-blue suit from Savile Row, the gold watch-chain strung across his waistcoat subtly emphasizing the fine cut of his bespoke jacket. With his thick main of silver hair combed straight back, his distinctive grey sideburns, his strong, masculine jawline, and his cold, penetrating eyes enhancing the confident portrait he presented of himself, he embodied his title: "The Gold King" did indeed stand before us.

Sam Clemens also wore a dark, well-tailored suit, but his appearance was not nearly as grand. It didn't matter, of course. Regardless of how he dressed, that unruly hair, those tufted eyebrows, and the dark moustache instantly demanded attention.

"Mr. Clemens," said I, "we didn't know you were coming. It was only when our page announced your name just now—"

"Your *page*?" he interrupted with his high-pitched Southern drawl. "Why that boy ain't much bigger than a paragraph."

Politesse made me chuckle even though I recognized the pun from Clemens' novel about the Yankee in King Arthur's court. At the same time, I was thinking how it didn't matter that these two men had presumably come to discuss a tragedy; in his public persona, it was quite obvious that Sam Clemens could not escape the role of jester.

The Senator, on the other hand, remained stoic.

I introduced Sherlock Holmes to Clemens, and the writer did the honours for his friend.

"Mr. Holmes," said Clemens, puffing out his chest, "allow me to present to you the Honourable J. Neil Gibson, a former

American Senator from one of our great western states."

We all shook hands, and Holmes, indicating the patterned sofa, proffered cigars. Both visitors seated themselves but declined the tobacco. Knowing Clemens' penchant for smoking, I took his refusal to be an indication of the gravity of the visit.

"Jed," said Clemens, patting the Gold King on his knee, "let me get this confab started."

In spite of his desire for urgency, Gibson nodded in resignation. Having already heard the relish with which Clemens told a story, I reasoned that Gibson must have believed the writer would begin with or without the Senator's approval. Gibson moved Clemens' hand away from his leg, and I remember thinking that the Senator would have allowed no one else such familiarity.

"Gentlemen," said the writer, "not too long ago, I had the good fortune of entertaining my old friend Jed here, along with the late Mrs. Gibson, their two children and governess at Dollis Hill House just outside of London, where my wife and daughters and I have been spending the summer. Dr. Watson, I've already told you how the Senator and I originally met."

"In the Gillis cabin on Jackass Hill," I put in, as proud as any student correctly answering an examination question.

"By way of introduction, let me say that the Gibsons were planning to join us last month at Dollis Hill. The thing is, it was about the same time I was supposed to offer up a few words at the dedication of the new Reading Room of the Kensal Rise Library. It's right near the house, and I never miss a chance to praise a place where people can get their 'mental food'. But when I saw that the ceremony would interfere with the Gibsons' visit—well, I was going to withdraw my services. That's how much I anticipated their stay. Yet the Senator here would have no part of my plan. As soon as he learned I was fixing to back out of the speech, he rearranged his entire schedule so as not to conflict."

"It was Grace's idea," explained Gibson.

"Grace Dunbar, your governess," confirmed Holmes.

"Yes," Gibson nodded. "She said that changing the family's plans in order to honour a library set a good example for the children." He put his head in his hands. "God," he cried, "that was before any of this bloody business ever occurred."

"Settle down, Jed," Clemens cautioned and patted him on the knee once more.

"Sam," said Gibson, "just tell Holmes why we're here. We're running short of time."

Sam Clemens smiled. "Sure, Jed. I just wanted Mr. Holmes to know how close our families are." However serious the reason for their visit, it was clear that the information would be delivered according to Clemens' schedule and no one else's.

"Actually, Mr. Holmes," said the writer, "the Senator is correct. Time *is* of the essence. Today is Thursday; my family and I sail for America on Saturday. Obviously, our trip back home requires a great deal of preparation. Right now, we're staying at Brown's Hotel over on Albemarle Street, but we're still in the middle of packing things up out at Dollis Hill. We'd just moved over to Brown's when Jed came to me with the terrible news about Maria—a real tragedy that you may already know something about—and it requires immediate attention. From what I hear of your talents, I'm hoping you can resolve the issue before we leave England."

At last, Clemens had got round to the death of the Senator's wife. It was just as Holmes had anticipated; and with his suspicions confirmed, he turned to the Senator.

"Without knowing the exact nature of your difficulty, Mr. Gibson," said Sherlock Holmes, "I promise no results. What's more, regardless of your friend's entreaties or travel plans, I certainly promise no timetable for resolving matters that have not as yet been made known to me."

The American author folded his hands, raised his luxuriant eyebrows, and sighed.

"Sam," demanded the Senator, "just get to the point."

"Indeed, Mr. Clemens," Holmes echoed, "please *do* get to the point."

"Perhaps I *will* have that smoke now, Dr. Watson," said Clemens. Gibson emitted a frustrated snort. I fetched the cigars from the coalscuttle near the fireplace and offered one to Clemens. After biting off the end, he lit up, closed his eyes and inhaled.

After giving the rest of us the momentary opportunity to exchange impatient glances, he opened his eyes again—the storyteller gone, replaced by the concerned friend. "As a detective, Mr. Holmes, you probably know that the Senator's wife has been cruelly murdered."

"I am aware of the crime, Mr. Clemens. She was found shot dead some two weeks ago on Thor Bridge, which is, as I understand it, a stone construction spanning Thor Mere on the Senator's property in Hampshire."

Brief as Holmes was in describing the scene, the Senator covered his face with his hands again and slowly shook his head.

"I am also aware," continued Holmes, ticking off on his fingers each fact as he announced it, "that no gun was found near the body; that what appears to be the murder weapon was discovered in the wardrobe of the governess, Miss Grace Dunbar; that the gun, which has the same calibre as the bullet extracted from Maria Gibson's skull, had one round expended; and finally that Miss Dunbar has been apprehended and, as we speak, sits in the Assizes at Winchester awaiting trial by jury."

Clearly impressed by my friend's knowledge, Clemens raised his shaggy eyebrows again. At the same time, the Senator sat with wrinkled forehead, its furrows having deepened at Holmes' description of the governess' fate.

Just then, the casement windows began to shake. It was as if Aeolus himself had blown upon them, and Gibson started at the rattle.

The wind continued for several minutes, but Sherlock Holmes ignored it. "Come, come, Mr. Gibson. I gleaned all the details I mentioned from the newspapers. Surely, if this murder brings you to my door, there must be additional facts which have yet to be made public."

The proud face of J. Neil Gibson reflected only agony.

"Let us be frank, sir," said Holmes, bringing his hands together. "If you have no new information regarding your wife's murder, one is forced to conclude that the quick apprehension of the guilty party must be the cause of your current distress. It is logical to assume that you have a particular interest in the imprisoned Miss Dunbar. One hears she is quite an attractive woman."

There's no need to reproduce the dialogue that I already reported in my original account of these events. I copied those words accurately the first time I wrote about the case. It may well be that Marlow Bates' wild allegations had pointed my friend in the right direction, but it was Sherlock Holmes himself who accused the Senator of harbouring romantic designs on the young governess whilst Gibson's wife still lived.

The Senator flushed, and the wind ceased its howl.

In the silence that followed, Holmes made clear to the Senator what he wanted to know: "Describe for me, Mr. Gibson, the exact nature of the relations between yourself and Miss

47

Dunbar."

The man looked more likely to pounce on Holmes than to answer to him. Clenching his fists, Gibson breathed deeply and narrowed his steel eyes. All he did, however, was to stand up, grab his hat and coat off the rack, and bolt from our rooms.

"I'll fetch him back," said Clemens with a wink.

In my original account, I had falsely attributed Gibson's return to the guilt he felt over being asked to confess his interest in Miss Dunbar. At the behest of Conan Doyle, I did not report that it was due in great part to the encouragement of Sam Clemens that Gibson made his sheepish return.

"You were right, sir," the Senator admitted to Holmes once we all re-seated ourselves some fifteen minutes later. "Although it's not something I'm comfortable discussing with others, I do love Miss Dunbar with all my heart; and while I mourn the death of my wife, it tears me apart to think of poor, innocent Grace sitting in a gaol cell. I don't know what I was thinking just now when I walked out, Mr. Holmes. Sam reminded me that it was your reputation in resolving such matters that convinced me to come here in the first place. I should never have left like that, and I will spare no expense in helping you find a way to clear Grace's good name."

In response, Holmes walked across the room to the table where his scrapbook lay open.

"Senator," he said, motioning for Gibson to join him, "this is my file volume titled "G". I would like you to peruse the newspaper accounts I have already collected related to the murder of your wife." Holmes leaned down to flatten the pages where he had pasted his most recent acquisitions.

The Senator shrugged and got up. Joining Holmes at the table, he began to peer at the neatly displayed white cuttings.

Strange, I thought, *Holmes seldom reveals his research to the public.* I could only assume that he was showing off his files on this occasion to confirm his interest in the case or to corroborate Sam Clemens' high regard for my friend's detecting skills.

Whatever Holmes' intention, Gibson's cursory glance reflected how unimpressed the Senator was. I wasn't surprised. After all, one could easily deduce from Holmes' earlier restatement of the case that none of the cuttings revealed anything new. Still, the Senator did pick up the volume, and soon he was reading not only the numerous journalistic accounts of his wife's violent death but also the blatant suggestions of his own romantic entanglements with the governess. Perhaps he had not realized how many different newspapers were reporting the story, or maybe it was just the allure of reading about himself that had caught his attention. Whatever the reason, once he'd begun, he stood mesmerized by the newspaper stories before him.

It was only after Holmes had left Gibson on his own to review the files that I realized the scrapbook presentation had nothing to do with any *braggadocio* on Holmes' part. Rather, the diversion allowed Holmes a few moments with Sam Clemens. In fact, as soon as Gibson appeared engaged, Holmes leaned over to whisper into Clemens' ear. It took but a minute or two for them to exchange confidences.

Shortly thereafter, Gibson concluded his survey of the scrapbook pages. "You're right," he said to Holmes. "There's nothing new here. But at least your collection convinces me that I've come to the right man."

Holmes rubbed his hand together in anticipation. "Early this afternoon, I shall go to the Lord Chancellor's Office to secure the legal papers that will allow us to speak with Miss Dunbar at the Winchester Assizes. Afterwards, if Dr. Watson agrees, he and I shall travel to Hampshire to arrange the interview."

My afternoon was free; and, if necessary, a nearby locum could be counted upon to look in on my surgery for the next day or two. I nodded my approval.

"Thank you," said Gibson. "You're both welcome at Thor Place. Since you'll be occupied for the next few hours, I'll return home immediately and prepare to welcome you this evening." He turned to his friend. "Sam?"

"You know I wish I could help you more, Jed; but you're in good hands with Sherlock Holmes. As matters stand though, I've got to get back to Dollis Hill to help Livy and the girls finish packing things up. You know we're returning to the States the day after tomorrow. We've been off traveling for years, and there's still a lot to take care of. Why, you don't know how much convincing I had to do just to arrange the free time for this morning."

Gibson nodded, presenting what for him might have passed as a smile. "Thanks for what you've done so far, Sam. You got me here. Now that I've met Sherlock Holmes, I have hope for Grace's freedom." Suddenly, he slammed his right fist into the open palm of his left hand. "By God!" he thundered, "I may even find out what really happened to my wife!"

"Hold on a minute, Jed," said Clemens, obviously caught up in the Senator's exuberance. "Let me find out if I can take care of our family business sooner than later and maybe tag along with Mr. Holmes and Dr. Watson when they travel out to Thor Place. If I can make it, I'll see you later."

The two men slipped into their overcoats; and after exchanging words of encouragement and handshakes with us, they departed.

No sooner did I hear the front door close downstairs than

I turned to Holmes. "What did you say to Clemens?" I demanded to know. "I saw you whispering when Gibson was examining the cuttings."

"Bravo, Watson!" Holmes exclaimed as he replaced the scrapbook amongst the other volumes on the shelf. "Your powers of observation grow by the day! I did indeed whisper to Clemens. I asked him if we might talk alone once the Senator had gone, and Clemens invited us both to Dollis Hill House this afternoon. We agreed that our meeting would be brief because he really does have travel-matters to attend to while he's there. But he said that he could discuss the case at the same time he was undertaking his familial responsibilities."

I moved to a front window and pulled back the curtain. The wind had died down some, but I could see our departing guests bending forward against it as they negotiated the short distance to the curb. Each then hailed a separate hansom—one to convey Gibson to Waterloo for the train to Hampshire, the other to take Clemens to the Baker Street station for his seventeen-minute journey back to Dollis Hill.

"I stand ready to join you, Holmes," I announced. "Both to Dollis Hill and then to Thor Place."

"Good!" Holmes exclaimed, clapping his hands and edging toward the fire. "I thought you might be particularly eager to pursue this investigation. Solving a murder has its own kind of attraction, but I assume that a writer like yourself would also find additional value in spending more time with Samuel Clemens.

Holmes certainly knew how to engage me. The only perquisite he'd left out was the usual: gaining more material for future narratives. After all our years together, however, he was well aware that such a proposition went without saying.

I sat pondering the upcoming journey whilst the wind

began rattling the casements again.

Part II

On the Hunt

Chapter Five

If you don't want [detectives] to find out about a thing,
it's best to have them around when you do it.
--Mark Twain
"A Double-Barrelled Detective
Story"

Dollis Hill House and its environs lived up to the idyllic description that Sam Clemens had offered at Nevill's. In just a matter of minutes, the train from Baker Street had whisked Holmes and me away from the choking air and teeming crowds of central London and deposited us amidst the green hills and flowery groves of Dollis Hill, a halcyon countryside where even the winds had ceased to blow.

The solitary redbrick house sat on a low-lying hillock in the midst of a six-acre park. Engulfed by the russet hues of copper beeches and antique oaks, Holmes and I soon found ourselves at the gentle incline of the gravel drive, which we followed to the entrance, a wide, squared-off portico framed by tall, narrow, white-trimmed arches. The portico's flat roof was enclosed by wrought-iron, Italianate-style railings; and an outdoor chandelier hung from its ceiling. To the right the entry, a square tile offered a bell pull. This convenience proved unnecessary, however, for the door stood ajar.

"Shall we?" said my companion, motioning towards the open portal.

Our unannounced arrival gave me pause, and I hesitated.

"It's not as if we're invading someone's hearth, old fellow. Officially, the Clemens family are no longer in residence; they're living in a hotel in central London."

I shrugged my shoulders and followed Holmes inside.

From the entry hall, we could perceive the disarray. Crates and trunks dominated the drawing room and library. Most of the containers bore labels signalling "Removals and Warehousing Department"; but some read "Harrods"; and others, "Army and Navy Stores". Many of the boxes remained open, and a few of the large trunks gaped wide, their hungry drawers pulled out as if waiting for more clothes or *bric-à-brac* to consume.

With no sense of a destination, we began inching our way along a maze-like path amidst the containers. Happily, before we'd proceeded too far, a maid in black uniform came to the rescue.

"Our Virgil come to guide us," I cried with relief.

The poor woman looked puzzled, but Holmes offered her our names. "We are expected," he added, and she responded by pointing us at a French window that led to the veranda.

Just outside the doorway, we discovered the Clemens family rigidly poised. Behind them in a gentle decline sprawled a lawn of emerald green. Photograph-like, they stood ready to greet us—Sam, at the centre in a white, rolled-brim straw hat; his wife Olivia and their two adult daughters, Jean and Clara, at his sides. In the background, beyond the waves of pink foxgloves, thick shrubbery and towering trees, an ocean of verdant hills rolled off into the distance, their green rises sprinkled with white sheep and yellow haystacks.

"You'll join us for tea, gentlemen," said Olivia Clemens, a short, slight woman dressed in a frock of dark-grey. Her words were in the form of a request, and yet they maintained the ring of command.

It didn't matter that we were hoping to solve a murder. Or that Holmes had to get to Westminster for the papers to admit us to see Grace Dunbar. One look at the table—its white linen tablecloth already bedecked with ivory-coloured plates, silver tea service, and assorted cakes and biscuits—informed us that there would be no arguing with her plans. Our trip to Hampshire later that afternoon was going to be delayed.

"Please excuse the chaos inside, gentlemen," said she with a brief but courteous smile. "All that you see is the result of the Clemenses waiting too long to start their packing."

"Fortunately," added her husband, "we are sailing on a 16,000-ton ship, which should be large enough to accommodate all our possessions."

The two daughters rolled their eyes.

Sam Clemens persisted in his humour, but the atmosphere throughout our socializing seemed tinged with a kind of melancholy. Jean and Clara occasionally split the quiet with trills of musical laughter befitting the offspring of a great comic wit, but both daughters were clothed in dark hues from head to foot— Clara in navy-blue, Jean in burgundy with a black scarf round her neck.

It was the family doing their best to appear unbowed. At Nevill's, Sam Clemens had already alluded to the death of the eldest daughter Suzy, who had died of spinal meningitis at the age of twenty-four at their home in Connecticut. At the time, the rest of the family had been touring in Europe, and the tragic news had staggered them.

Four years had passed since the catastrophe, and yet the Clemenses still seemed struggling to overcome their loss. Worse still, Suzy's death seemed to corroborate a sense of familial doom.

Many years earlier, their first-born, a son named Langdon, had died before the age of two; and Jean, as we would learn later, was currently visiting a London osteopath three times a week for treatment of her epileptic condition.

As far as I could tell, the Clemens family fought for stability in their own ways—Sam through his writing, Olivia through her family, and both daughters through their desire for normality. With their hair swept up in the latest style of pompadour, both Jean and Clara appeared chic young women sensitive to fashion and culture.

"You could model as 'Gibson girls'," said I, hoping to lighten the mood. I was referring to the sketches of Charles Dana Gibson, the popular American illustrator whose world-famous portraits depicted the most sophisticated of modern women with their white, swan-like necks and swirls of dark hair piled high on their heads.

"Thank you," said Clara; Jean blushed.

Not to be outdone, Clemens quipped, *"Jed's* the only Gibson I can think of who'd come calling on these girls."

Jean rolled her eyes again, but Clara cast a stern look in her father's direction. The tension evaporated temporarily when Mrs. Clemens invited us to the table. Once we were seated, Clara proceeded to pour the tea.

We sampled lemon cake, shortbread and ginger biscuits, yet how Mrs. Clemens found such delicacies amidst the mayhem of moving has remained a mystery. Following our repast, Sam Clemens appropriated a cigar from the round humidor on the wicker table to his right and offered Holmes and me a smoke. With business and travel still to be completed, we waved off the invitation. Clemens, however, would not be deterred and, biting off the cigar's tip, spat it on the grass, and lit up. Within moments, as if attracted by the pungent aroma of tobacco, a longhaired white cat bounded onto the lawn. It had entered the garden from a break in a nearby hedgerow and, silently padding over to Clemens, began rubbing its flank against his leg.

"I love cats," sighed the writer, bending over to pull the animal into his lap. "This one isn't ours. He just likes to visit." Stroking the white fur, Clemens observed with admiration, "When you dress in white like this fella, you get noticed." He rubbed behind its ears. "And lots of affection."

"Dollis Hill House is a historic locale, is it not, Mrs. Clemens?" asked Sherlock Holmes.

Holmes wasn't one to prolong social chit-chat, especially since I knew how desirous he was of getting to Thor Place that afternoon. But his every action had a purpose, and I recognized how he was cultivating Mrs. Clemens. Slighting the woman by rushing through her carefully planned family tea might interfere with securing whatever cooperation Holmes might need later from her husband.

It was Jean who answered, however, her dark eyebrows knotted in seriousness. "You're quite right, Mr. Holmes. The house used to be the country seat of Lord Aberdeen."

"It was frequently visited by his friend Mr. Gladstone," added Clara, "your former prime minister."

I had to smile at the young American's identification of a name all Englishmen would immediately recognize.

"We were told that Mr. Gladstone appreciated the clean air," said Jean softly, "and that he liked morning swims in the pond."

Clemens pointed at a tall scotch fir. "He's said to have planted that tree in honour of Queen Victoria's Golden Jubilee in 1887."

Turning, Clemens gestured at the greensward that extended gently downhill to a small, round pond. The water was partially hidden by tall grasses, but one could still espy most of the white and yellow pond lilies that floated on its surface.

"I reckon Gladstone had good taste," said Clemens. "The pond's a favourite spot for Mrs. Clemens and the girls."

"Mr. Gladstone used to string a hammock between two large trees down there," said Jean. "We did the same." More quietly, she added, "Now, it's all packed away."

"How did you describe the scene?" Mrs. Clemens asked her husband. "'Divinely beautiful and peaceful', wasn't it?" She looked sadly out over the low hills. "I'd like to stay here forever, Youth," she sighed.

"'Youth'?" I questioned.

"My pet-name for Sam," said she. "It captures his vitality. Maybe I think he'll stay young forever if I keep calling him that."

Clara thought for an instant. "There's a woman we know, Miss Isabel Lyon. She met Papa a number of years ago playing whist. She has another nickname for him. She calls him 'the King'. *Mama* would never use such a term, but Senator Gibson likes it. He says it gives him royal company—'the Gold King' and Papa. They call themselves 'the two kings'."

"I'll stick with 'Youth'," Mrs. Clemens smiled—beamed, actually. Let others think of him as a 'King'."

I understood Mrs. Clemens' point. There was already too much counterfeit royalty running round; the world had much more to gain from the vitality and naiveté of youth. Besides, I could perceive that she had a way of directing her husband. Sam Clemens might bask in fame's light, but both he and his wife seemed to understand that—at least, within the bounds of their household—he was not all-powerful.

"Livy watches out for me," Clemens said as if sensing my thoughts. "I read my manuscripts to her—most of them, anyway."

She shot him a warning glance.

"She acts as my censor. She understands what readers will tolerate and what they might find offensive. Of course, living with me has familiarized her with all kinds of language—both the acceptable and the other."

"Oh, Youth," Mrs. Clemens said with a blush.

"One time," Clemens went on, "I cut my chin shaving and let fly a host of oaths. Worse, I discovered that I'd left the door to the bedroom open."

"Oh, yes," his wife smiled.

"I still had the hope that Livy was sleeping and hadn't heard my profanities, and I tried to sneak away without having to pay some sort of moral fine. I didn't even look to see if she'd heard me; but by the time I'd tiptoed to the door, I couldn't take not knowing. I just had to turn around to be certain she was still asleep. Asleep? No siree, not Olivia Langdon Clemens. No, she was sitting up in bed—her hair down to her shoulders and her hands folded in her lap. Do I need to say that she looked like an angel?"

"And then," Mrs. Clemens put in, having ignored her husband's compliment, "I slowly repeated word for word every one of the profanities Youth had uttered."

Sam Clemens' cheeks flushed. "What I said then, Livy, still holds true: you got the words right; you just couldn't carry the tune."

He and his wife looked at each other. It was obvious that they shared a mutual affection. Clara and Jean seemed to understand it as well. They let silence underscore the depth of their parents' feelings. The only sound was the purring of the cat.

Finally, Clara pointed to a particularly luxuriant section of lawn. "We used to lay a rug on the grass out there and read and sleep. It's so much more relaxing than Brown's Hotel. I know we haven't been home in such a long time, but it's still a shame that we have to give up this place."

"True," observed Clemens. "Oh, Brown's is nice enough. It has all the modern inconveniences. I do believe its elevator was a gift from William the Conqueror. But as for Dollis Hill, I think it comes nearer to being a paradise than any other home I've ever occupied . . . ."

The declaration hung in the air for a few moments, as if offering all of us yet one more opportunity to appreciate its aptness.

"Really," Clemens said, "the only thing wrong with Dollis Hill is that Livy doesn't know how she's ever going to leave it." And he and his wife exchanged another obviously long-practiced look.

"There's also no telephone," Clemens added.

He seemed about to start in on some new tale related to the electronic device when Sherlock Holmes suddenly clapped his hands together. The white cat's ears shot up at the sound.

"Mr. Clemens," said Holmes, "I need to remind you that we have a crucial journey to Hampshire on our schedule. And before that, I still must pay a visit to the Permanent Secretary in the Lord Chancellor's Office."

Mrs. Clemens understood immediately and got to her feet. "Youth," she announced, smoothing down her skirt, "the girls and I are going inside to make sure the packers have everything in order. You all must do what you can to aid Senator Gibson."

Holmes and I also stood, and Mrs. Clemens addressed the two of us. "So nice to have met you, gentlemen," she said, offering each of us her hand.   Clara and Jean smiled and followed their mother into the house.   The white cat, which had already taken the opportunity to leap from Clemens' lap, raised its tail and paraded inside after the ladies.

"Wherever Livy is," said Sam Clemens as he watched his wife disappear through the doorway, "there is Eden."

Sherlock Holmes sat down again, and I followed suit.

"Now, Mr. Clemens," said Holmes cutting directly to the matter at hand, "it's time to get back to business.   I have some questions to ask.   If you would, tell me how you assessed Senator Gibson's marriage.   He *is* your old friend, after all."

Clemens took a final pull on his cigar and then snuffed it out in the square glass ashtray on the wicker table.   He shot the smoke into the air. "Jed was in his thirties when he met Maria down in Brazil; like me and Livy, he was ten years her senior. 'Course, he was extremely wealthy by then; his gold mines had paid out considerably.   Maria was young, beautiful and full of fire." Beneath his raised eyebrows, he offered us a wink that any man could understand.   At least, he'd waited for his wife and daughters to depart before alluding to such indelicacies.

"In the beginning, Jed was quite taken with her; and not much time passed before they married and he brought her back to the States."

"And once they returned?"

"That was when Jed decided to run for the Senate.   He'd always been interested in politics.   Don't forget that he'd gone to law school before he went out west.   With his reputation as a common man who'd struck it rich—not to mention his educational background and good looks—he was a great favourite among the political class and wound up getting elected.   He was also a great favourite among the women—always has been, even now—just like in the old days in the Washoe when he rendezvoused with all sorts of ladies. 'Course, back in the early days of those mining camps in Nevada and California, there was usually just one *kind* of lady who came around—if you get my meaning." Here he winked again.

"He must have realized they were simply after his money," said I.

"Not back in California; in those days he didn't have much. Later, there were plenty of bankers and lawyers around to remind him."

"Not to mention his wife," said Holmes.

"Ah," smiled Clemens, 'there's the irony. I think Jed began to believe that *every* woman was after his money—*including* his wife. And so he pushed her away. When our families visited earlier in the summer, Jed and Maria scarcely appeared together except at dinner when it was expected they should."

"They did find the time to have two children," I offered.

"Which brings us to the governess, Grace Dunbar," said Holmes.

Clemens smiled again. "A beautiful girl who'd been hired to teach the Gibson children—which, as I understand it, she did admirably well. But you see, gentlemen, Jed fell for her the first time he laid eyes on her. As a result, he pushed his wife even further away and led Grace on. I do believe he told her he'd divorce Maria, but I don't think he ever really would have. The mother of his children? No sir, I don't think he would have done that."

"If that's the case, you seem to be suggesting that the only way for Miss Dunbar to have elevated her status in the Gibson household was to eliminate her rival."

"Damn!" Clemens ejaculated. "It does sound like that. And

yet I don't mean it that way. Grace Dunbar is an independent and sensitive young woman. Reminds me of my daughter Suzy. Strong-willed. Concerned. Why, Grace got that tightwad Jed Gibson to contribute to charity. To give money *away*! She had him wrapped around her finger."

"But he wouldn't leave his wife," I put in.

"No," Clemens agreed, "he wouldn't. It may sound silly under the circumstances, but he believed in the old-fashioned ideal of standing by the woman he'd married—however much he might love another."

Clemens' faith in Gibson's sense of tradition was noble, but it did nothing to diminish Miss Dunbar's motive for murder—to rid herself of competition for the affluent Senator's hand.

For a few moments silence blanketed us as we contemplated the ironies, and then we all agreed we had to get moving. Before we could set off for Hampshire, however, Holmes still needed to obtain approval from the Lord Chancellor's office to meet with the imprisoned governess. Sam Clemens, I assumed, would also need extra time at home to impart his final instructions to the packers.

"I've already spoken with Livy," the writer surprised us by saying, "and she said she can do without me till tomorrow evening. So with your permission, gentlemen, I will accompany you to Thor Place. If you can complete the paperwork regarding our visit to Miss Dunbar, Mr. Holmes, we could meet at Waterloo at 4:00."

A few hours later, with the official permit admitting us to see Grace Dunbar in my colleague's hand, Clemens, Holmes and I were clattering southward along the rails towards Hampshire.

Chapter Six

Well, a detective don't ever ask a question right out about what he wants
to know. He asks questions away off yonder, round about, you know,
that don't seem to bear on the matter at all, but bless you they're deep—
deep as the sea. First thing a man knows, that detective has got all the
information he wants, and that man don't ever suspect how he done it.
--Mark Twain
Simon Wheeler, Detective

The railway journey to Hampshire seemed a race with Helios' chariot. We had left the confines of London late Thursday afternoon with the sun above us; upon our reaching the boundaries of the city, sunlight still bathed the slate-roofed housetops and their grimy chimney pots. Though shadows grew longer, the sun continued to shine upon the sweeping green hills and tall, thick forests through which the tracks cut; upon the rolling fields with their white sheep and stippled Herefords; upon the rambling meadows with their yellow honeysuckle, purple prickly-heath, and greens and browns of pigweed.

"'The Copper Beeches'," murmured Sam Clemens, interrupting my appreciation of the glorious English panorama.

"Sorry?"

"In your narrative, 'The Copper Beeches'—you described making this trip before. You and Holmes were going to investigate some villainy here in Hampshire at a country house called 'The Copper Beeches'."

I nodded at the recollection. Personally, I had travelled this line on numerous occasions; but I had reason to write about making the journey with Holmes only once. Ironically, in the investigation to which Clemens was referring, we had also been coming to the assistance of a governess. In spite of the singular unpleasantness of the case, I recalled enjoying the quiet Hampshire countryside through which, like today, our train had been racing. On that journey too my musings had been interrupted—by Holmes himself.

"Don't be fooled, Watson," he had observed as I looked out the window. "It is but a beguiling landscape you admire. Never forget that evil can flourish all the easier in the isolated houses of the countryside."

I'd looked at him in disbelief. *How can the charms of nature evoke such dark thinking?* I'd wondered. *How can Holmes harbour so anti-Romantic, so anti-Wordsworthian, so anti-British a thought?* My incredulous stare must have rattled him, for he rationalized his pessimism as the simple curse of a suspicious mind. I took him at his word, and yet here we were again—on our way to bucolic Hampshire to investigate another act of evil.

Helios had steered his chariot low in the sky since we'd left London. As it turned out, our trip to Winchester had taken more than two hours; and it was much too late for our interview with Grace Dunbar. In my original account, I had attributed our tardiness to bureaucratic entanglements; but the more accurate reason was that Holmes and I had spent too much of the afternoon socializing at Dollis Hill House. As a result, we would have to postpone the meeting at the Assizes until the next morning. To alert Senator Gibson of the change in plans, we directed to Thor Place the stationmaster's son, a helpful lad of ten;

and the Senator responded via the boy with an invitation for the three of us to retire for the night at the estate.

Sam Clemens had visited the manor before, but for Holmes and me the first glimpse of the half-timbered, part-Tudor, part-Georgian structure came during our approach in the trap we'd hired at the railway station. With the setting sun now casting pink streaks on the swathes of clouds beyond it, the grand house, situated as it was on the rise of a low hill, presented a most dramatic silhouette.

We rolled to a stop on the gravel drive not far from the entrance. Clemens and I followed Holmes out of the carriage; and in the cool fall air, the three of us crunched our way the few paces to the flags and the massive oak door. Its large bronze knocker was shaped like a wreath, and Holmes lifted it and let it fall, producing a loud, muffled clang. He repeated the action, and the door was opened—not by the butler, as we had expected—but by the rude Mr. Marlow Bates, the same nervous American whose off-putting visit to Baker Street earlier that day had preceded the arrival of Senator Gibson. Equally surprising, instead of inviting us in, Bates actually exited the house, quietly pulling the door closed with his right hand before approaching us.

Motioning Holmes and me aside, he whispered conspiratorially, "Gentlemen, I beg you not to mention to the Senator anything I told you earlier about giving him my notice." From beneath a frown, his eyes glanced at Clemens; but before anyone could respond, Senator Gibson himself swung open the huge door.

"What's going on out there, Bates?" Gibson asked. Without waiting for an answer, he summoned us into the large entry hall and immediately turned to Holmes. "Time is of the essence," he insisted, "so let us not stand on formalities. We must proceed as quickly as we can in defence of Miss Dunbar. Every minute we delay is a minute longer she remains locked up."

Holmes nodded. "I'll need to speak with the local authorities first. Who would that be?"

"Sergeant Coventry," said Gibson. "He's not one of those Scotland Yard types you're probably used to, Mr. Holmes, just a village constable; but he handled the investigation."

"In light of my experience with Scotland Yard, I'm much more inclined to place my bet on the village police."

"I agree," said Sam Clemens though I reckoned that his observation was based more on philosophy than experience.

"Good," said Gibson. "I'll take you to see him myself."

"No," Holmes replied. "It will be more efficient if I conduct this investigation without the interested parties looking on. Senator, you and Mr. Bates should remain here."

Bates was about to protest Holmes' rejection, but the Senator cut him off.

"Fine. Whatever you say. But take Sam; he'll provide another set of eyes."

Holmes nodded although I suspected that the last thing he wanted was a talkative writer looking over his shoulder.

"You'll need to go to Coventry's cottage," Bates put in. "It serves as the local police station. It's only a brief walk from here."

"Excellent," said Holmes. "We'll just check our rooms and then—"

But before Holmes could complete his sentence, Clemens burst into a spasm of loud coughs. He needed to place his hand against the wall to steady himself. "Water, Bates," he somehow managed to gasp. "A glass of water."

The wages of too much smoking. I enjoyed a good cigar as much as the next man. But Sam Clemens, who claimed to have been born into the world asking for a match, was rumoured to smoke some twenty cigars a day. Strange to say, however, the coughing lapsed when Bates left the entry hall and resumed only after the nervous young man had returned with a cut-crystal glass of water.

Clemens nodded in appreciation as he drank.

Once the writer had controlled his coughs, he retired to his room still carrying the glass. Holmes and I retired to the rooms Senator Gibson had set aside for us and prepared to face an autumnal Hampshire evening. I donned bowler and overcoat; Holmes, deerstalker and Inverness cape. I was rummaging through my Gladstone for a scarf when Holmes confirmed my earlier suspicions.

"I would have preferred excluding Clemens from our meeting with the police," said he softly, "but bringing him along at least should keep Gibson in line."

"I understand," said I, and the two of us returned to the gravel drive at the front of the house.

For the next quarter of an hour, Holmes and I found ourselves pacing up and down as we waited for Clemens. Eventually, appearing no worse for wear from his coughing fit, he ambled out clad in a big coat and followed by Gibson. I assumed Clemens must have left the water glass somewhere in the entry hall.

"I just wish I knew the cause of his ruse," muttered Holmes.

I had no chance to ask Holmes what he meant before the two men reached us. Pointing off in the darkness to a path between some oaks, the Senator provided us with the instructions for our short walk; and Clemens, Holmes and I marched off in the direction of the trees.

The sergeant's cottage—police headquarters, if you will—turned out to be a small, rustic structure of light brick, weathered beams, and thick ivy. It was well after working hours, yet the constable still remained in his uniform. Judging from the stack of police bulletins under the gas lamp on his desk, I imagine that he had been thumbing through the latest official reports before getting up to answer our knock.

Tall, thin and balding, Sergeant Coventry presented a sepulchral image at the door. And yet from the warmth of his welcome and the earnestness of his gaze, one could perceive how appreciative he was to meet a famous writer like Samuel Clemens. The extreme vigour with which he shook the hand of Sherlock Holmes, however, revealed that sharing detective work with my renowned friend was even more appealing.

"Mr. Holmes," said he, "your reputation precedes you." As we immediately discovered, Sergeant Coventry possessed the maddening habit of occasionally dropping his voice to a whisper. Yet in spite of swallowing the final few words of his salutation to my friend, the policeman's sentiment was obvious.

Coventry paid close attention as Holmes explained the purpose of our visit—how he, Mr. Clemens, and I were there to re-examine the murder of Mrs. Gibson with the intent of finding new evidence that would exonerate the governess.

"With all due respect, Mr. Holmes," replied Coventry, "as much as I'd like to report otherwise, I've come across nothing that might help free the woman."

Holmes responded with a single request: "Take me to where Mrs. Gibson's body was found."

With the aid of a dark lantern, Sergeant Coventry was only too pleased to escort the three of us down another gravel path, this one leading to a small bridge of grey stone that arched Thor Mere. Despite the looming darkness, one could see that the bridge—broad enough to serve in the main carriage-drive— consisted of Italianate balustrades on either side topped with waist-high parapets of grey stone. The mere itself was shaped like an hourglass with the bridge at the narrow centre separating the water into two large lakes. The surfaces of both were clogged with reeds, and I can remember thinking how very difficult it would be even in daylight to locate anything that had fallen into so murky a mess.

"Show me exactly where the body was found," said Holmes to Coventry as we approached the stone structure.

The policeman directed the light of the lantern to an area at the far end of the bridge not more than twenty paces beyond us. The murder was weeks old, yet dark stains could still be seen where Mrs. Gibson's blood had pooled—presumably, the same spot where the poor woman had encountered her killer, Grace Dunbar.

I was quite used to my friend's methods; but Sam Clemens and Sergeant Coventry gawped in fascination as Holmes, asking Coventry for the dark lantern, did his best to scrutinize the scene. Holding the lantern high, he looked up the drive that led to the great house just under half a mile away, then down the drive in the opposite direction leading to the high road well beyond his range of vision, and finally the tall, thick hedgerow that paralleled the lie of the bridge. Next, he held the lantern over the parapet and leaned over as far as he could to look into the water; then, moving to the point directly opposite, he repeated the procedure.

"Pah!" Holmes exploded, still bent over the side. "There's

nothing to see—not in this light anyway. The water's too deep, and these infernal reeds conceal whatever might rest below."

"Perhaps in the daylight," Clemens suggested, but Holmes simply stood up and brushed the dirt from his hands.

"No, there's nothing more to be seen down there."

"Whatever can he be looking for?" asked Sergeant Coventry. "The only object of note that might possibly have been thrown into the mere is the pistol." *Sotto voce,* he added, "And it's already been found in Miss Dunbar's wardrobe."

"Though the *dead* may tell no tales," mused Sam Clemens, "a *gun* can reveal many secrets." In an apparent afterthought, he observed, "Perhaps I shall write a monograph on the subject."

Whether this comment was intended as a sarcastic echo of an oft-spoken statement by Holmes, my friend paid him no mind. Instead, Holmes returned his attention to the spot on the bridge where the unfortunate woman had fallen. He was particularly careful to direct the light at a small chip of exposed stone he'd discovered at the bottom of the upper lip of the parapet, just above the balustrade. The nick couldn't have been more than a shilling in size; but especially in the beam of the lantern, the fresh whiteness was impossible to overlook.

Kneeling at the balustrade, he took out his lens and with the aid of the lantern studied the chip through the magnifying glass. When he'd concluded his observations from various angles, he applied his fingers to the indentation, touching it here and there, feeling all of its properties.

"Sergeant," Holmes asked, "do you recall seeing this nick before the murder?"

"'*Before* the murder'? Can't say as I do. But I did note it during our investigation, and I remember thinking that it looked newly made."

Holmes now placed the lantern on the ground where Mrs. Gibson's body had lain and then, producing a tape from somewhere inside his cape, measured the distance between the lantern and the nick on the parapet.

Sam Clemens stroked his chin. I thought I heard him utter the word "gun" once more as he begged our leave and strode purposely up the path and back to the house.

Holmes never looked up. He appeared fascinated by the chip, which he continued to examine. Then picking up the lantern, he repeated his action of holding it over the railing and leaning out as far as he could—save this time carefully positioning himself directly before the small blemish in the stone.

"Blast those reeds!" he shouted after a few moments. "I can see nothing."

Following his words of frustration, he stood up straight and returned the lantern to the policeman. "Sergeant Coventry," he announced, brushing *débris* from his hands, "I thank you for your help."

Coventry's eyes widened at the abruptness of his dismissal. Nonetheless, he saluted Holmes, nodded in my direction, and proceeded to glide away toward his cottage. He may have uttered some form of farewell; but if he had, I didn't hear it.

"Watson," said Holmes as the constable's footfalls diminished on the gravel, "we shall return to the house. I hope to convince the Senator to arrange a carriage to transport us to Winchester tonight."

"Tonight?" I had assumed we'd be making the trip together in the morning when we were to conduct our interview with Miss Dunbar.

Holmes flashed one of his enigmatic smiles. "Since we

have so little time at our disposal, we should complete any official business regarding our visit with Miss Dunbar as soon as possible. Staying in Winchester tonight will allow us to present the Lord Chancellor's papers early in the morning. When Gibson and Clemens arrive, we may begin our enquiries immediately."

"And the gun that was found in Miss Dunbar's wardrobe? Do you not intend to examine it?"

Sherlock Holmes displayed his all-knowing grin. "No need, Watson. That gun was an innocent bystander and has nothing to offer. If need be, we can take a look at it tomorrow after we return from Winchester." Extending an arm in the direction of the house, he indicated our route back.

I had not taken more than a step when Holmes put a hand on my shoulder and whispered in my ear, "Did you see him, Watson?"

"Who?"

"Bates—the estates manager."

"Where?"

"Standing behind the hedgerow near the bridge. I noticed him in the beam of light as I turned to examine the mere, and I've been keeping an eye on him ever since. He returned to the house just after I suggested you and I do so."

I was about to respond when suddenly Holmes hushed me. We were some thirty yards from the front door, which was now open. As a result, we could easily see the self-same Mr. Bates, his small frame silhouetted at the threshold by the light in the entry hall. He was facing Holmes and me; and when we approached him, he appeared most calm and collected—as if he had *not* just returned from spying on us—and yet his eyes seemed to smoulder.

No sooner did we reach the man than Holmes requested

the Senator's carriage for our trip to Winchester. "And, Bates," he added, "please convey to the Senator that we would like to meet him at 9:00 tomorrow morning at the Assizes."

"Certainly," the American said and was gone.

In darkness, Holmes and I waited for the carriage at the front steps. At that moment, Sam Clemens stepped out the front door. He was now smoking a long cigar.

"And did you learn anything from the gun?" Holmes asked. His wink in my direction indicated how trivial he regarded this line of investigating.

Clemens nodded in the affirmative, exhaling a cloud of rich smoke at the same time. "The gun belongs to Jed. He's got quite a collection. This one's a pearl-handled Smith and Wesson rimfire .22 with an octagonal barrel and a spur trigger—one of a pair, I'm told. They're made by the Whitney Armoury in Connecticut."

"You seem quite familiar with such weaponry," I observed.

"One doesn't live long enough to achieve manhood in the silver fields of the Washoe, Doctor, without gaining that kind of knowledge. Out there, being uneducated about guns can be fatal."

"Anything else?" Holmes asked, his tone *blasé*.

"I reckon we'll just have to wait and see," Sam Clemens replied cryptically.

At that instant, a clatter of hooves announced the arrival of our transportation—a smart growler, its side-lanterns burning, pulled by two bays. Clemens accompanied Holmes and me out to the carriage and watched as we climbed in among the rich dark-leather and polished-brass fittings. The driver applied the whip, the growler lurched forward, and in spite of his gout Clemens managed to trot a few steps along side the rolling vehicle to wish us well.

"Remember!" he shouted, "I must return to London by

tomorrow evening!"

I offered him a wave; and an instant later, Holmes and I were rattling down the drive toward the high road.

"We'll stay at the Black Swan once we get to Winchester," said Holmes. "If you recall, it's not far from the station in the High at Southgate Street."

"The inn where we met the governess all those years ago."

"The same. Not the most accommodating of hotels, but certainly one of the most practical."

I remembered the establishment. Above its entrance posed the statue of a black swan with wings outstretched. It was at a table just inside the door that Miss Violet Hunter had shared with us her concerns about the mysterious activities she sensed at The Copper Beeches.

The carriage bounded on, and I turned to look through the back window at Senator Gibson's grand manor house. From our current vantage point, however, all I could discern in the darkness was the round, red glow of Sam Clemens' cigar.

Chapter Seven

What is wanted is genius and penetration and marvelousness.
A detective that had common sense
couldn't ever make a ruputation [sic]—
couldn't even make his living.
--Mark Twain
"Tom Sawyer's Conspiracy"

Winchester, the ancient capital of Saxon England, was blanketed by heavy grey clouds Friday morning. The foreboding sky rendered all the more gloomy the fortress-like structure of the Assizes. Yet the threatening heavens seemed fitting as Sherlock Holmes and I paced anxiously among the shadows of the medieval structure. To the prisoners within—as well as to their defenders without—the thick stone walls and thin high windows underscored the same discomforting conclusion: any poor wretch entombed within had little chance of ever gaining freedom.

Some two hours before the Senator was scheduled to arrive, Holmes had presented to the authorities the transit papers he'd acquired in Westminster. With the documents assuring us access to Grace Dunbar in order, we had every expectation that our meeting with her would face no difficulties.

What we didn't expect was the entourage that accompanied J. Neil Gibson. The pounding hooves of the bays announced the arrival of the Senator's coach; but after the Gold King and Sam Clemens descended from the growler, we were also surprised to see a tall, ginger-haired young man emerge. Senator Gibson identified him as Mr. Joyce Cummings—the barrister in the defence of Miss Gibson. I was about to whisper to Holmes that at least Marlow Bates hadn't made the trip when a pale hand reached out from the darkened interior of the carriage to gain support on the japanned-wood doorframe. The hand, we immediately discovered, belonged to the diminutive figure of the estates manager.

"Surely we have too large a crowd!" I exclaimed. "We will drown the poor lady in a sea of humanity."

"Watson is correct," said Holmes, immediately taking charge. "We must limit the number who enter the gaol." Holmes nodded in the direction of each man as he announced who would meet with the prisoner: "You, Senator, Gibson; you, Mr. Cummings; you, Watson; and myself. Mr. Clemens, Mr. Bates, please do us the honour of waiting out here."

"I will have a smoke," declared Sam Clemens.

Bates, however, was not so easily put off. Dismissed by Holmes for a second time now, he narrowed his eyes and clenched his fists.

"See here, Mr. Holmes," he snarled, "I've travelled a good distance to see Miss Dunbar. I don't plan to be shut out now."

"Bates!" the Senator commanded. "You heard Mr. Holmes. You'll wait out here."

Bates took a step forward, and the Senator placed a hand on the young man's shoulder. Their angry glowers eerily mirrored each other.

"Do you not take my meaning?" Gibson asked. "What's the matter with you?"

Bates continued to glare at his employer, opening and closing his fists.

"Yes?" Gibson demanded.

Clearly, Bates had not yet told Gibson of his intention to leave the Senator's employ. If Bates had so informed him, I'm certain Gibson would have sacked him on the spot. As it was, we left Clemens seated on a wooden bench puffing away on a long cigar that tilted upward at a jaunty angle. As for Bates, he remained standing on the front steps of the Assizes stewing in his anger.

The rest of us entered the prison.

Holmes showed the Lord Chancellor's permit to a short, heavily-moustached man in a business suit. He'd already read the paper earlier that morning and, acknowledging the presence of Senator Gibson, turned us over to a uniformed turnkey standing nearby. The officer proceeded to lead us down a long, dark corridor between facing rows of heavy oak doors. The cluster of keys at his belt jangled as he walked.

At the end of the corridor, he stopped before another heavy door upon which he knocked loudly. It was opened by a stern-faced wardress attired in black. The turnkey murmured something in her ear; she nodded, and bade us follow her into the wing of cells reserved for women prisoners. She too had an impressive set of keys, but neither they nor the rustle of her dress could drown out the intermittent cries we heard emanating from behind the doors on either side of the walkway.

In defence of our social system, greater minds than mine have argued that even the most idealistic of utopias will eventually require the maintenance of prisons. Still I must confess that the thought of the fairer sex being driven to crime— let alone having to submit to incarceration—makes me question the kind of society we have created. I am not naïve; I do know of women like child-murderers Frances Kidder and Ann Lawrence here in England and Mary Surratt, conspirator in the assassination of President Lincoln in America, who were hanged for their heinous acts; but I have to believe that there must exist more humane ways to treat even the most demented of females than leaving them to the rope.

The dankness in the narrow corridor threatened to envelop us, and yet we had to travel the entire length before the wardress stopped at the end of the passage.

"In here," said she, pointing at the ominous portal before us. Then she reached for the keys at her waist and slowly sorted among them. Finding the key she was looking for, she fitted it into the lock; and we heard the click as the mechanism disengaged. Slowly she pulled open the thick wooden door and gestured for us to enter the cell in which Grace Dunbar had spent the last two weeks. We stepped into darkness, and the wardress pushed the door shut and locked it from the outside.

There was poor lighting from the small, barred window near the top of the back wall, but one still could see her beauty. In spite of the compulsory dull-grey muslin gown with its stitched broad arrow, the plain white apron, and the white pillbox cap that hid much of her brunette hair, one easily perceived that Grace Dunbar was a striking woman. It was, however, a frightened face that first confronted us. Like a captured fox, she bore the look of one who recognizes she's at the mercy of superior forces.

Yet when Gibson suggested she sit on her cot, she refused; and with her dark eyes suddenly flashing, she stood tall in the gloom. One could well understand how a powerful man like J. Neil Gibson had been drawn to a defiant beauty like this governess.

My original account of the tragedy on Thor Bridge recorded the questions and answers exchanged between Grace Dunbar and Sherlock Holmes in her cell: Yes, she had written the note that was found in Mrs. Gibson's dead hand—but it was only in response to Mrs. Gibson's request for written confirmation that Miss Dunbar had penned a reply at all. Yes, the Smith and Wesson had been found in her wardrobe, but she had no idea how it had got there or how Mrs. Gibson had come to her death. Yes, she had tried to dissuade the Senator's advances. Yes, she had known of the dislike she had engendered in Mrs. Gibson—"hatred" was the term the governess employed—and as a result, yes, Miss Dunbar had kept her distance from the Senator's wife. Indeed, as long as Senator Gibson was married, the governess encouraged no romantic approaches from him; and following her rebuff of his initial crude attempt, no such behaviour on his part manifested itself again.

"Quite clearly," Holmes observed, "your life at Thor Place was tainted with hostility."

"It is true, Mr. Holmes," said she, looking directly into his grey eyes. "And yet, in spite of my initial discomfort, I assure you that I have killed no one."

Holmes returned the stare, as if taking her measure. "Why did you not simply leave?"

Miss Dunbar allowed herself a quick smile. "Most people regard Neil Gibson as a rich tyrant; I suppose I pierced his armour. I told him that there was no need to build his empire on the backs of ruined men; and do you know that for whatever his reasons, he listened to me. He began by supporting the charitable causes I espoused, and slowly he seemed to understand that a man of his high status could be highly influential in making the world a better place. I never believed that I was his sole motivation. Truth be told, I thought he might be atoning for some dark secrets in his past. But whatever inspired him, I couldn't walk away—as long as he didn't try to make our relationship any more personal."

If it was possible, Grace Dunbar stood even more erect as she uttered this last pronouncement; and I thought she could not look any nobler. Despite the gloom of her oppressive cell, I saw her pale face gain colour and her nostrils flare. Frightened but unbroken before the penal system, she voiced a declaration of innocence that rendered her utterly heroic.

Unfortunately, we had little to offer this proud woman. Without any new evidence, Mr. Cummings was left to describe the bleakness of the case against her; and the Senator, to issue words of sympathy. Only Sherlock Holmes presented her a hint of optimism.

"I still have my investigation to conclude," said he.

Grace Dunbar caught my friend's final word. "'Conclude'? You're not finished then, Mr. Holmes? Might I take that as an offering of hope?"

Holmes cocked an eyebrow, displaying the flicker of an enigmatic grin. "One last question, Miss Dunbar," was all he said. "Would you happen to know anything about how there came to be a chipped stone in the parapet of Thor Bridge?"

"I know nothing of a 'chipped stone', Mr. Holmes. Whatever can you mean?"

Holmes dismissed her query with the wave of his hand. Then he slapped the thick door to signal we were ready to leave. We heard the wardress disengage the mechanism; and Holmes, encouraging Miss Dunbar to keep strong, motioned for us to adjourn.

Only the Senator held back. Leaving the cell, I glimpsed him in the gloom grasping Miss Dunbar's hands and offering her a reassuring smile. "We'll get you out of here, my darling," said he in a low voice. Then he too left her, and the wardress swung the door shut, the segments of the heavy lock coming together with a loud clang. We retraced our steps down the dark corridors, breathing more easily only when we reached the outdoors.

Upon our exit, Bates emerged from the shadows; and Clemens, tossing away his cigar, got up from his bench.

"Any news?" Bates demanded. "Has she anything convincing to say of her innocence?"

"*She* has nothing new to say about her innocence, Mr. Bates," answered Sherlock Holmes. "But one may certainly hope that *I* shall produce some new conclusions along those lines once I revisit the scene of the crime in the light of day."

Marlow Bates regarded Holmes with wary eyes—as if, in spite of the long list of Holmes' successful cases, Bates had no reason for sharing my friend's confidence, however slim. All Bates could offer was a weak, "I hope you're right, Mr. Holmes."

"Now," declared Holmes, "I must re-examine Thor Bridge."

For his part, Mr. Cummings set off down the High Street. As counsel for the defence, he maintained an office in Winchester and had additional legal matters to discuss with local members of the bar regarding Miss Dunbar's case.

That left five of us packed inside the Senator's carriage: Holmes and I faced Gibson, Bates, and Clemens. Before we began to move, however, Holmes leaned his head out the window.

"Driver!" he shouted. "Find the nearest post office."

The growler plunged forward, and we all looked to Holmes for an explanation of his request.

"I must send a wire to Sergeant Coventry," said he cryptically.

* * *

"What are your intentions?" Gibson asked Holmes once

we'd all stepped out of the carriage into the brilliant sunshine in front of the manor house.

'Gentlemen, I have an experiment to conduct. I'll thank you to leave Dr. Watson and me alone so we can complete it. Have no fear. In due time, we shall furnish you with the results." Without waiting for questions, Holmes turned, and I followed. Quickly, he grabbed my arm. "Watson," he whispered, "I assume you've brought your revolver."

I usually did so on such occasions. "My Webley," I confirmed. "It's in the Gladstone in my room; I thought it inappropriate to bring a gun to the Assizes."

"Quite right," said he. "But fetch it. We'll need it when we arrive at the bridge."

With that, Holmes turned on his heel and marched down the path to the mere. I nodded in the direction of the three gentlemen, and withdrew to my room to retrieve the pistol. *Why a pistol in these friendly confines?* I wondered. *Are we in any danger?* With such questions confronting my mind, I hurried off to join Holmes at the water's edge.

Chapter Eight

Truth is stranger than fiction,
but it is because fiction is obliged to stick to possibilities;
truth isn't.
--Mark Twain
Pudd'nhead Wilson's New Calendar

I caught up to Sherlock Holmes at the mere. The bright afternoon sky had replaced the dark clouds of the morning, and a blinding brightness reflected off the still surfaces of the two large pools. I had to shield my eyes to discern Sergeant Coventry on the bridge at the narrow centre. Like a centurion guarding a key passage over some strategic waterway, the uniformed policeman presented quite the heroic portrait, save that the sword he should have been holding upright against his shoulder was, in fact, a long-handled fishing net.

"I brought it, Mr. Holmes," the sergeant said, raising the net in question when we'd reached him, "just like you requested." He voiced my own concerns when he added softly, "Though I can only fancy what sort of fish you hope to catch with it."

Holmes flashed his enigmatic smile. "Follow me," he commanded, and the policeman and I strode after him. A few steps later, he stopped directly in front of the curious chip in the stonework.

"Watson, your pistol, if you please."

"Now?" I cried. *Not a villain in sight!* To what use could he put it?

"An experiment, Watson." He gestured with his open hand that I should give him the Webley. "I'll supply the twine."

I knew better than to question Holmes' plans; and removing the gun from my pocket, I carefully placed it in his palm.

"This should do nicely," said he, hefting the Webley to sense its weight. Happily, he removed the bullets before slipping it into his jacket. Then he turned to Coventry. "Sergeant, the twine?"

"Here it is, Mr. Holmes," said the policeman, offering my friend a ball of straw-coloured string. "Stout cord from the village shop, just as your wire requested." He swallowed that last bit about the wire, but it was clear to me that the instructions to the sergeant comprised the content of Holmes' telegram from Winchester.

The policeman and I remained mystified as Holmes extracted a small knife from an inner pocket and proceeded to cut a six-foot length of twine. He tied one end round the butt of my gun and then slid the pistol inside his coat again. Next, he walked to the end of the short bridge and off onto the verge. He scanned the ground for a few moments before stooping over and fumbling amongst the large black rocks at his feet. One at a time, he employed both hands to pick up a few of the bigger stones and tested their weight.

"This will do quite well," said he at last and returned to the bridge with a rock the size of a large potato.

From inside his coat, Holmes now produced my Webley with the twine tied about its handle. Securing the free end of the cord round the stone, he tied a double-overhand knot to prevent any slippage. Next he leaned over the parapet and, holding the gun in one hand, used the other to slowly reel out over the water the six feet of twine with the stone at the end. In such a manner, he was able to lower the stone a few inches at a time, stopping when the rock dangled a yard or so above the mere. Between the handle of the gun he was holding and the heavy stone hanging over the balustrade, the line pulled taut.

"Regard," said he, turning to face us. Then to my utter horror, he held the gun to his temple.

"Holmes!" I shouted, forgetting the chamber was empty.

"Bang!" he shouted back and, opening his long fingers, let go of the gun—as would have occurred had he actually shot himself. We all heard the stone splash into the water. The gun, secured to the rock by the twine, flew after it, but not before knocking into the upper edge of the bridge's parapet less than an inch to the right of the pre-existing chip. It then flipped over the top and, like the stone that was pulling it, disappeared into the murky depths.

Sergeant Coventry let out an appreciative whistle.

"Suicide, gentlemen," said Holmes triumphantly. "Mrs. Gibson cold-heartedly planned her own death to incriminate her bitter rival, Miss Dunbar. Clearly, Mrs. Gibson was confident that the gun wouldn't be found beneath the thick blanket of reeds under the bridge—so confident, in fact, that she had previously planted a weapon of the same calibre in the governess' wardrobe. With one of its chambers emptied—Mrs. Gibson probably fired it harmlessly somewhere out in the woods—the Smith and Wesson rimfire .22, the gun found in Miss Dunbar's wardrobe, perfectly fit the role of the murder weapon. And yet, as this little demonstration reveals, we may now perceive that the second gun was merely the innocent mate of the weapon that actually performed the deadly deed, one of a pair, which—as we have previously learned—belong to the Senator."

"Bravo, Holmes!" I cried. "You have cleared Miss Dunbar!"

"Not yet, Watson. We need evidence." Holmes turned to Coventry. "The final proof is awaiting *your* discovery, Sergeant. Be so kind as to use that fishing net to locate Dr. Watson's Webley; I should be very much surprised if Mrs. Gibson's Smith and Wesson is not submerged along side it. Bring them both to the house when you find them."

"Right you are, Mr. Holmes," Coventry said with a reassuring salute. Then he made his way to the water's edge and parted the congestion of reeds with the rim of his net.

"Now, Watson," said Sherlock Holmes, rubbing his hands together in anticipation, "while the sergeant puts the final touches on the investigation, let us report our findings to the Gold King himself."

As we began walking up to the large house, we saw Marlow Bates striding towards us. In a great hurry, he barely acknowledged Holmes or me as he continued on towards the bridge.

"Can I be of any help?" I heard him ask Coventry.

Sherlock Holmes seemed unconcerned with the convenient appearance of the estate manager, so I disregarded it as well. After all, Holmes had convincingly demonstrated that the dead woman had committed suicide. About what else was there left to worry?

* * *

No sooner had Holmes and I arrived at the front door than the butler delivered us to the library, a magnificent, wood-panelled room framed by ceiling-high, cherry-wood shelves fully stocked with books. To our surprise, however, it was not Senator

Gibson we found seated at the large mahogany desk at the centre, but Samuel Clemens. The Senator himself was pacing the dark-blue carpet, stopping every now and again before the cavernous fireplace, its flickering flames mirrored in the gilt-imprinted spines of the leather-bound texts surrounding us.

Clemens was holding a single open volume. Its boards were maroon-coloured; and though it too had gilt lettering, the title was too distant to make out from where I was standing.

"What news, gentlemen?" asked Gibson impatiently.

"Most encouraging news," announced my friend.

The Senator offered a cautious smile. Till this very moment, he'd heard nothing to provide the smallest bit of optimism regarding the case against Grace Dunbar.

"I can safely assure you, Mr. Gibson," said Sherlock Holmes, "that Miss Dunbar is innocent. That much I have demonstrated."

Gibson stopped in his tracks and brought his hands together. "Thank God, Mr. Holmes," said he, still hesitant to display even the most cautious of smiles. "But are you certain?"

"Although we await Sergeant Coventry's confirmation, I am quite convinced that Grace Dunbar did not kill your wife. In spite of appearances to the contrary, I'm afraid that in reality Mrs. Gibson committed suicide."

"Suicide?" Gibson repeated, eyes wide. "But how is that possible? The police found the gun in Grace's room."

"Your late-wife, it would appear, prepared so devious a plot that it would result in Miss Dunbar's being accused of the murder."

Sherlock Holmes recounted his view of Maria Gibson's vengeful plan, emphasizing both her clever dispatch of the gun on the bridge and her planting of its mate in the governess' wardrobe.

Gibson stood speechless. Clemens, however, narrowed his eyes, keeping open the book he was holding.

"It is," said Holmes, "one of the more ingenious schemes I have ever encountered."

Just then Sergeant Coventry appeared at the library door. In his arms, he cradled a small number of bulky objects concealed beneath the folds of a thick, white towel. With obvious concern for the thick carpeting, he slowly lowered his load to the floor and carefully opened the towel. On the white cloth before us lay two large black stones of similar size, both wrapped in lengths of twine. At the end of one strand lay the Webley, which I had lent to Holmes. More importantly, at the end of the other lay the true murder weapon, the Smith and Wesson rimfire .22 that had killed Maria Gibson.

"Capital!" cried Holmes, the only one to utter a word, astonishment having gripped the rest of us.

Suddenly, two significant sounds erupted. One was the terrible thunder of hooves. Framed through the library window was the diminutive figure of Marlow Bates astride a large chestnut mare galloping down the drive towards the road.

The other was a cynical "harrumph" that emanated from Sam Clemens. It drowned out the slap made by the book he was holding when he'd slammed it shut.

We had no clue as where Bates was off to in such a hurry, but we certainly had Sam Clemens within arm's length to explain his explosion of displeasure.

"A very good job of detecting, Mr. Holmes," growled the writer, his bushy brows angling together, his blue eyes focused sharply on my friend. "But I reckon it's not good enough."

My jaw dropped. Even his Scotland Yard rivals offered

Sherlock Holmes more respect.

"You dare challenge my conclusions, Clemens?" Holmes shot back. "Dr. Watson and Sergeant Coventry found quite convincing my demonstration that not only explained the chip in the bridge wall, but also produced the very gun with which Mrs. Gibson took her life. Here it lies before us." Holmes pointed to the pistol in question and then brought his hands together. "I'm sure you'll agree—a most compelling argument for freeing Miss Dunbar."

"Yes, Sam," added the Senator. "Mr. Holmes' conclusion is precisely what this investigation has been about from the start. It's the reason we went to Baker Street in the first place. Mr. Holmes' discovery confirms that Grace—Miss Dunbar—could not possibly have been my wife's murderer. And for such thinking I am truly grateful."

"I too am pleased to see that this evidence clears the governess," said Clemens. "But it falls short of identifying the true killer."

Holmes, Gibson, Coventry, and I all exchanged glances.

"In the case of a suicide," said I, "it goes without saying who the culprit is."

In spite of the severity of his claim, Clemens' blue eyes twinkled. "Gentlemen," said he, nodding towards the window where we'd just seen horse and rider shoot past, "while you quibble, the actual murderer is making his escape."

"Bates?" Gibson questioned. "Surely, you're barking up the wrong tree there, Sam. Maria shot herself. The gun that Coventry fished out of the water proves it. There's no reason to question any other suspects. And certainly not that pissant Bates."

Sam Clemens raised his formidable eyebrows, continuing

to gaze out the window.

Sherlock Holmes thought for an instant. "Marlow Bates is a very odd fellow," said he. "I'll grant you that much, Clemens. But no matter how dramatic the timing, riding off on a horse does not constitute a murder confession—especially not after we've identified the shooter as the victim herself."

Sam Clemens harrumphed again. "Suit yourselves," said he, "but the man you want is getting away."

"*I'll* bring him in!" Coventry cried and turned towards the door.

"Not so fast, sergeant," said Holmes, stepping in front of the policeman to block his exit. "Before you arrest an innocent man, let's hear how Mr. Clemens defends his so-called reasoning. It shouldn't take very long."

"Dactyloscopy!" Sam Clemens announced. And he proceeded to hold up for all of us to see the book he'd been reading.

This time I was close enough to make out the title printed on the volume's spine: "Finger Prints." Smaller letters identified the author as Francis Galton. Immediately, concern about Bates' precipitous flight began to work its way into my head.

For his part, Sergeant Coventry was nervously rocking from one foot to the other.

"I discovered Galton in November of '92," Clemens said, tapping the book's cover. "I was writing *Pudd'nhead Wilson*, and Galton's observations got me so excited that I turned my plot into a kind of mystery story to be solved with fingerprints. At some point during the Civil War, I heard a German fella talk about a bloody thumbprint that'd led him to solving a murder. The subject's fascinated me ever since. Soon as I realized back at Dollis Hill that we'd be taking a second look at a murder, I brought along this copy of Galton."

"How very interesting," Sherlock Holmes said coldly.

"Thanks to Galton here," Clemens explained to my friend, "while you were examining the generalities of the crime scene, I was studying the specifics of the physical evidence—in point of fact, the Smith and Wesson found in Miss Dunbar's wardrobe. You've done an admirable job as far as you've gone, Mr. Holmes— I mean, proving Miss Dunbar's innocence—I'm sure we can all agree to that—but I'm compelled to point out that you have neglected to complete your investigation."

Sherlock Holmes took a step backward. He was not used to having his rational explanations challenged so blatantly.

"I know a thing or two about fingerprints myself, Clemens," he fired back. "In this case, they don't apply. Bertillon has taught us much about how a rogue's physical make up can identify him as a criminal, and hands are only one component of the portrait. What's more, as Watson can tell you, I too have made use of finger-marks. There was that bloody thumbprint in the investigation Watson called 'The Norwood Builder'. And there are others. Which cases am I forgetting, Watson?"

As soon as Clemens had mentioned finger-marks, I'd begun riffling through the archives in my brain where I keep the cases of Sherlock Holmes filed away. I was his Boswell, after all, and therefore had to be prepared to answer: "You looked for, but couldn't find, incriminating fingerprints in the case of 'The Three Students'; there was a dirty thumb-print that led to nowhere in 'The Man with the Twisted Lip'; and, of course, there was that thumb-print on the letter to my late wife Mary in *The Sign of Four.*"

I realized full well that none of those examples involved identifying a perpetrator based on specific prints. Indeed, I believe Holmes must have come to the same conclusion. Yet I kept quiet on the subject, and he would not let down his defence.

"There," said he defiantly. "Do you see, Clemens? Of course, I know of such things. Do you take me for an illiterate? I am well aware of advances in fingerprint analysis—including those of your friend Galton, whose work I too have read and whose lecture on fingerprinting I personally attended two years ago at the Royal Institution on Albemarle Street. Funny you didn't ask me about Galton before—the hall where he spoke is only a minute's walk from your hotel. And I haven't even mentioned my familiarity with the techniques of identification utilized by Galton's predecessors like Herschel in India and Fauld in Japan. Perhaps it will be I who shall someday write a monograph on the subject. Don't admonish *me* for failing to rely on the latest forensic developments."

"In that case, Mr. Holmes," replied Clemens calmly, "I can only conclude that in this particular investigation you simply failed to put all your knowledge into practice. You neglected to use available fingerprints for identifying the true perpetrator. Identification is what Galton is all about. *Identification!*—not just pointing out that one person's whorls and ridges are different from someone else's."

Holmes arched his eyebrows, a clear sign of his indignation. But it was the policeman in the group who actually spoke up.

"I've heard enough," said Coventry. "My bicycle's at my cottage. I'll try to catch Mr. Bates at the train station in Winchester. It's his most logical route of escape." He swallowed his final words while managing to sidestep Holmes, and then he hurried out the door. We could hear his rapid steps fading on the gravel path.

"A trifle premature, I fear," commented Holmes coldly to no one in particular. "As you should know," he said directly to Clemens, "one needs a storehouse of fingerprint information to make such discoveries meaningful. Only when some agency creates a fingerprint library will one be able to announce with any degree of certainty whose marks belong to whom."

I understood what both men were suggesting, each with his own sense of righteousness. But knowing Holmes as well as I did, I also recognized how his vanity could get in the way of his accepting help from others.

And Clemens wasn't finished. "Mr. Holmes," said he, "I believe I already reported the admonition I once offered my wife. To you, I offer the same: 'You may know the words, but you can't carry the tune'."

Holmes' face turned florid; he clenched his teeth.

"Gentlemen, please," Gibson cut in, holding up his hands. "This is beginning to sound like an old-fashioned pissing contest."

"Not so fast, Jed," said Clemens. "Hear me out. Then you can decide for yourself what really happened to Maria."

Gibson nodded reluctantly; and in spite of an exasperated sigh by Holmes, Clemens opened a desk drawer and removed from it a white handkerchief wrapped round a small, cylindrical object. Carefully, the writer extracted a familiar-looking glass of cut-crystal from inside the folds of linen—the same glass Clemens had got from Marlow Bates during his coughing fit the night before. Holmes had suggested at the time that Clemens' paroxysms had been a ruse. Now we learned the reason: the coughing attack had been cleverly staged to secure Bates' finger-marks.

"Allow me to explain," offered the writer.

"Go ahead," said Holmes stiffly.

"Not up on Galton, the murderer would have no reason to cover his hands. Thus, I anticipated finding fingerprints on the gun in Miss Dunbar's wardrobe. And after examining its barrel and handle, I found what I was looking for. Luckily, since I had no reason to suspect the servants, there were only a few significant people to check—Jed here, his estate manager Bates, and Sergeant Coventry, who'd kept the gun found in the wardrobe under lock and key. It was child's play to gain the Senator's finger-marks. They're all over the house. And Coventry was most helpful when I explained that I needed his prints to ease the confusion caused by any strange marks. To be certain I got an accurate set for Bates, I'm afraid I resorted to an old-fashioned con. "

"And where is all this leading?" Holmes demanded.

Clemens produced a cigar from inside his coat. "Since no one else but me and Sergeant Coventry, who's already gone after Bates, seem alarmed that the murderer is escaping, I believe a Cuban cigar would be in order." Yet again he was to delight in prolonging the account.

We stood round exchanging looks whilst Sam Clemens struck a Vesta, pulled on the long cigar, and exhaled a ring of smoke. The cloud rose slowly towards the ceiling, and he stared at the ring as if he had nothing else on his mind.

"Mr. Clemens!" an exasperated Holmes finally shouted. "We await your findings."

"Ah, yes," the writer sighed. "Business sometimes does get in the way of a good smoke. "

From Holmes' pronounced jawline, I could tell that he was about to explode.

Clemens now employed the cigar as a pointer, which he directed at my friend. "You were quite right to deduce an act of suicide, Mr. Holmes. For that's just what Marlow Bates wanted you to think—but only if the murder charge against Grace Dunbar collapsed."

"To what end?" I wanted to know.

"Indeed, Clemens," Holmes said. "What was Bates' motive?"

"Beyond protecting himself," the writer said, "I can't be certain of his motive. Maybe he was jealous of Mrs. Gibson. Maybe he was jealous of Miss Dunbar. Maybe he wanted to hurt *you*, Jed. I can't really say. What I *can* assure you of, gentlemen, is that Marlow Bates' fingerprints are all over that Smith and Wesson. He went to great lengths to make it *appear* that poor Maria had killed herself. But she didn't, you see? She was, in fact, murdered—only not by Grace Dunbar."

As we took in this revelation, Sam Clemens paused to pull on his cigar once again. "The way I figure it," he said, blowing more smoke toward the ceiling, "Bates encouraged Maria to stage that meeting with Miss Dunbar at the bridge and to be sure to get written confirmation of the fact. We know how—at Maria's own request—Miss Dunbar wrote that response agreeing to meet with her.

"With no love lost between them, the two women ended up in a shouting match, which Bates interrupted when he came on the scene. He waited for Miss Dunbar to leave; and then he, and *not* Maria, held the pistol to her head. He'd previously tied the ends of the string to the stone and to the gun handle just as I saw *you* do from a distance, Mr. Holmes. All that remained was for Bates to fire the weapon. Once he did, he just watched as Maria fell to the ground and the Smith and Wesson sailed into the water—but not before striking the bridge—as Mr. Holmes so admirably demonstrated."

We stood in silence conjuring the horrible tableau of the

counterfeit suicide.   Clemens had to be correct.   Bates had obviously wanted to destroy both women, not to mention Senator J. Neil Gibson.

Sherlock Holmes remained in contemplation for a minute or two. Then he walked over to the mahogany desk and, bowing his head, extended his hand to Clemens. I could only imagine how much effort it required for Holmes to make such a move.

"Mr. Clemens," said he softly as the two shook hands, "you have got the better of me. Let us hope that Sergeant Coventry catches up to the villain. In the meantime, we should search Bates' room. I'm sure you'll agree that the authorities have a way of corrupting possible clues whenever they search for evidence."

With Senator Gibson in the lead, we ascended the curved central staircase of Thor Place and followed him into the personal chamber of the estate manager. Bates had obviously left in a hurry, for there seemed no sign of a last-minute dash to collect his personal belongings—at least, not as far as a cursory look revealed. His clothing remained in place; his desk seemed in order. The entire room appeared neat and organized although—for all we knew—he might well have been keeping a valise at the ready in case his nefarious scheme had been discovered in its infancy. But that speculation was put to rest when, upon a more thorough search of the desk drawers, Holmes discovered a false bottom beneath a stack of estate papers.

In the secret compartment lay an old magazine. At first glance, the tattered pages suggested that it lacked any distinction, and yet the magazine had been important enough for Bates to hide. It turned out to be a copy of *The Overland Monthly*, an American publication dated August 1868 and edited by Mr. Bret Harte, an author I have already had occasion to mention in this narrative. In point of fact, amongst other articles within the oft-turned pages was Harte's own short narrative, "The Luck of Roaring Camp", the very story of a baby raised by California miners that back at Nevill's Turkish Baths Sam Clemens had called Harte's best work. As if to show ownership of the magazine, the name "Thomas Luck" had been scrawled next to the masthead at the top of the front page.

Puzzled anew, I stood staring at those yellowed pages. Did Bates' ancient copy of *The Overland Monthly,* apparently belonging to someone with the odd name of "Luck", have a connection to Senator Gibson or to the murder of his wife? I'm certain Sherlock Holmes was already contemplating an answer. But no sooner did the Hampshire constabulary arrive—alerted by the ever-reliable Sergeant Coventry—than they confiscated the magazine along with anything else in the room that they deemed consequential.

Part III

The Luck of Hope Canyon

Chapter Nine

Titles of honor and dignity once acquired in a democracy, even by
accident and properly usable for only forty-eight hours, are as
permanent here as eternity is in heaven.
--Mark Twain
Autobiography

In the end, Samuel Clemens couldn't say no to his familial
responsibilities. He left Holmes and me at Thor Place late Friday
night and rode the train back from Winchester to London. The
following day, the sixth of October 1900, he sailed with his wife
and daughters for America aboard the steamship *Minnehaha.*

Before going, Clemens had requested that I write him if
there were additional developments in the case. I readily agreed,
for one couldn't deny him any news regarding the *dénouement* of
a mystery he'd already done so much to solve. Thus, I awoke
early on the chilly morning of our first full day back in Baker
Street and arranged my writing tools on the small table in my
bedroom. Wrapped in a wool blanket, I proceeded to put down on
paper all that had transpired in the brief period since Clemens'
departure.

Most importantly, Grace Dunbar had been set free. With
Senator Gibson unwilling to allow her confinement to last even
one more day, her barrister, Mr. Cummings, presented the newly
discovered evidence to the Assizes in a special session on

Saturday. In deference to the Senator's high standing in the Hampshire community, the court was only too willing to accommodate Gibson's requests. Sergeant Coventry's presentation of the murder weapon, as well as the twine and the stone employed by Bates to ensnare Miss Dunbar, facilitated the legal transactions.

I was especially pleased to tell Clemens that no sooner had Miss Dunbar stepped out of the gaol than the Senator announced their intention to marry. I hastened to add that such news brought immediate delight to the Senator's young children, who, in spite of the loss of their mother, thrilled at the prospect of welcoming their beloved governess into the family.

Unfortunately, not all of the news was positive. I also had to report the unfortunate escape of the villainous Mr. Bates. The sergeant never did catch up to him. Initially, when Bates' chestnut mare—actually, Senator Gibson's—had been discovered that Saturday afternoon roaming the north Hampshire countryside, the police maintained high hopes of finding the man. The trail grew even warmer when railway workers on the Basingstoke platform of the London-bound trains reported seeing someone matching Bates' description earlier in the day.

By Sunday, however, these promising developments had led nowhere. In spite of Sergeant Coventry's telegrams to Scotland Yard describing the man in detail, no policemen positioned at Waterloo had seen him there—if, in fact, Bates had actually arrived at the station. And once the fugitive safely reached London, he could with a modicum of luck travel by rail to any destination in England. As a result, surveillance was increased at all the major railway stations. The police also promised added vigilance in patrolling the docks at Gravesend and other strategic ports like Southampton and Bristol, which were most likely to harbour ships sailing for America. The resources of the authorities notwithstanding, I was forced to end my letter to Clemens in ambiguity on the subject of Bates.

Nor did the news of Bates' escape sit well with Miss Dunbar.

"Must you leave, Mr. Holmes?" she had asked that Sunday afternoon as we prepared for our departure. "Mr. Bates is still at large."

"The house is well protected," Senator Gibson assured her. "The police will regularly stop by to check that everything is in order."

Amidst such optimism, Holmes and I offered our farewells. Miss Dunbar thanked us for our help and retired to the governess' room. Watching the Senator's *fiancée* gracefully mount the stairs, we recognized that soon enough she would be overseeing the entire household from that very same vantage no longer as a member of its staff, but rather as its mistress. I could only imagine that in spite of her humility Miss Dunbar must have been pondering similar thoughts.

"Time is of the essence," Holmes reminded Gibson once the governess had gone. "You were a politician. You know how these official investigations operate. The failure to negotiate a quick apprehension of Bates will diminish police interest in the man, and the hunt for the villain will lose its urgency."

The Senator was still relishing his victory over the Assizes, however, and not overly keen on being robbed of his triumph.

"Keep your shirt on," he said to Holmes. "Don't worry so much. I may not have been back to the States in years, but I still have connections. If Bates returns to America, my friends there will find him."

In fact, Gibson told us, one of his erstwhile business

associates, Henry Clay Frick, the former chairman of Carnegie Steel, had already cabled. The Senator had apprised him of the investigation's latest twists; and Frick had encouraged the Senator to contact the Pinkerton National Detective Agency in Chicago just in case Bates did reappear in America.

Sam Clemens had already told us how much he enjoyed ridiculing the "Pinks"; and given the dealings Holmes and I had experienced with the organization ourselves, relying on them gave me pause. To be sure, the agency's strengths were well established—they protected Presidents, after all. But so was the company's sinister reputation. Many people spoke ill of the Pinkertons for taking up arms against the workingman. Even in England, we knew the infamous story of their breaking the heads of steel workers some eight years before in Homestead, Pennsylvania, at the behest of no less a business titan than Gibson's friend Frick himself.

Now I'm not naïve enough to doubt that some labour unions can end up being commandeered by thugs. Only a few years before, I had reported just such a happenstance in the narrative I called *The Valley of Fear*. In that case Holmes and I had encountered a former Pinkerton agent called Birdy Edwards, who'd bravely infiltrated the Scowrers, a vile group of so-called workingmen, near the coalfields in the Vermissa Valley of Pennsylvania. Edwards, considered Pinkerton's "best man" at the time, helped destroy the entire murderous lot. Sad to say, the poor fellow ultimately disappeared at sea, probably killed as a result of his pursuit of justice. But not even the heroics of agents like Edwards could eliminate my reservations about the "Pinks".

"Whatever your politics, Watson," said Gibson, quick to recognize my hesitation, "the Pinkerton Detective Agency has an excellent record for tracking people down."

"Especially if they're enemies of big business," I muttered.

Gibson went on as if I hadn't spoken. "I'll wire them all the facts I have regarding Marlow Bates. At the very least, I'll instruct them to find out as much about him as they can."

"Keep us informed," Holmes said. "If news arrives that could shed light on Bates' whereabouts here in England, I'd like to offer my services in the effort to find him."

Having secured Gibson's pledge to share with us any relevant details concerning the missing Marlow Bates, Holmes and I boarded the train in Winchester for our journey back to London.

* * *

Completing my letter to Sam Clemens had delayed my arrival in our sitting room. I held up the envelope to Holmes by way of explanation for my tardiness. It was yet another morning that he had finished his breakfast before me and, though a fire blazed in the grate and I was just getting comfortable at table with the *Times*, my eggs, and toast, Holmes was preparing to leave.

Before he put on his overcoat, however, my eyes lit upon a small article at the bottom of the second page.

"Holmes!" I cried. "Have you seen this newspaper report of a break-in at the rooms of Bret Harte at Lancaster Gate yesterday?"

He nodded that he had and slipped his arm into a sleeve.

"It's so coincidental," said I, pointing to the report in question. "Wouldn't you agree? A break-in at Harte's home just two days after we discovered that magazine he'd edited, the one that Bates had hidden away?"

"*The Overland Monthly.*"

Holmes remained silent whilst I scanned the story. "Nothing was taken, it says. He seems to have frightened off his intruder."

"Do you know, Watson?—regarding the break-in?—I can't say that I'm surprised."

"Why not?"

"No time to discuss the matter now, I'm afraid," said he, grabbing a chequered scarf that had been hanging on the peg next to his coat. "I'm off to the British Museum to do a little reading. They're holding material for me, and I have an appointment to collect it."

I cocked an inquisitive eyebrow.

"I'll explain all upon my return." With a dramatic flair, he cast the scarf round his neck, positioned a short top hat on his head, and proceeded out the door.

I refolded the newspaper and placed it on a side table in case we needed it later. Then I summonsed Billy the page and handed him my letter to post.

* * *

Sherlock Holmes returned at 3:30 that afternoon. I remember the time so clearly because I'd been watching the clock since noon. It was at the meridian hour that Billy had brought up a provocative calling card addressed to Holmes. One glance at the name convinced me that the newspaper story about the disturbance at Lancaster Gate must have been connected to our recent activities in Hampshire.

Immediately upon my friend's arrival, therefore—even before he removed his hat and scarf—I pointed to the table near the door and announced, "That card arrived when you were out."

As a general rule, Sherlock Holmes was not a man to be hurried. Today, he seemed maddeningly deliberate. Slowly, he turned to hang his hat on the rack; laboriously, he unwound the scarf from his neck; tediously, he draped the scarf on its hook; painstakingly, he extricated first one arm and then the other from his coat. The coat too he had to put away before deigning to look at the card.

"I'm not surprised," he murmured once he'd surveyed both its sides. Then he sank into the armchair before the fire.

"Holmes!" I cried. "This is the second time today you've said you weren't surprised about matters that to me appear most surprising indeed. How can you be so *nonchalant*? That card is from the man responsible for the magazine Bates was hiding away." In truth, the card read:

Francis Bret Harte

Lancaster Gate

South Kensington

Written in tiny script on the back was the message: "Tonight, 7:30, No. 74."

"Sherry?" Holmes asked.

"Yes, certainly," I said in exasperation, "but what about Bret Harte?"

Holmes indicated I should sit opposite him, then rose and filled two small glasses with the amber liquid. "Watson," said he, handing over the drink and then re-seating himself, "it's not like you to become agog over celebrities. We've had actors, noblemen, even royals in our humble abode. This man is a mere scribbler."

His coarse comment evoked a tinge of anger within me. For a moment or two, I stared through the facets of the glass I was holding at a kaleidoscopic multitude of tiny fires dancing energetically in the hearth. Perhaps I sensed in Holmes' quick dismissal of Bret Harte a criticism of my own literary ambitions. How many times had Holmes complained that my sketches trivialized his displays of logic? And yet I also felt compelled to temper my irritation with the sympathy I held for Holmes himself. After all, the catalyst for his bitter words might be some lingering hostility from the wounds he'd suffered at the hands of another so-called "scribbler".

I sighed, took a deep breath, and tried again. "Why do you not seem surprised that Bret Harte has contacted you?"

"First, Watson," said he, "let me allay your fears. I *am* going to pay Mr. Harte a visit tonight, and I certainly hope you will join me."

"Of—of course," I spluttered, feeling silly not only for having thought Holmes to be criticizing me, but also for having raised a rumpus about the calling card in the first place.

As usual, Holmes seemed oblivious to my anxieties. "Allow me to answer your previous question with a question of my own."

I nodded, gesturing with my glass for him to proceed.

"Do you remember where I was heading this morning?"

"The reading room of the British Museum."

"And do you not have an inkling as to what I might have been doing there?"

Even though Holmes was clearly enjoying this game of cat-and-mouse, I knew I should have had an answer to his question, yet I was too mystified to produce one.

"Haven't the foggiest clue," I replied.

"Well, do you recall the magazine we found in Bates' desk?"

Immediately, I realized what Holmes had been up to. I

should have pieced it together earlier when he'd told me his destination. "*The Overland Monthly*," said I, "edited by Bret Harte."

"Quite so. They retain old copies there—all the way back to its beginnings in July of '68." Holmes paused to sample the sherry. "But Harte wasn't simply the editor in those days. Remember that he also contributed fiction—in particular, the short story called 'The Luck of Roaring Camp'."

"The story about the baby raised by miners. Sam Clemens mentioned it back at Nevill's."

"Yes, Watson. I am convinced that somewhere in that story there is a direct link to the murder investigation we just completed."

"And what do you suspect that link might be?"

"I have my suspicions, old fellow, which I am hoping can be confirmed by the editor and author himself."

I raised my glass. "To our visit with Bret Harte then," I toasted.

"Indeed," said Holmes and touched his glass to mine.

The ring of crystal echoed throughout the room.

* * *

Before meeting with Bret Harte, Holmes and I stopped in Maiden Lane for dinner at Rules. Seated in a booth of plush red velvet, we enjoyed not only a hearty meal of steak and kidney pie and sticky toffee pudding, but also the richness of the restaurant's ambiance. Numerous framed portraits and drawings hang amongst the lamps and hooks and dark-wood beams that interrupt the cream-coloured walls. Indeed, one can scarcely turn his head without sighting many an illustration by Leslie Matthew Ward, the acclaimed artist better known by his *nom de crayon* of

"Spy".

Perhaps it was Fate that surrounded us with all those caricatures. For after we'd hailed a cab and set off for Lancaster Gate, I realized that Spy's decades-old depiction of Bret Harte in *Vanity Fair* was prompting my mental image of the writer we were about to meet. In Spy's illustration, a dignified Bret Harte appears in tailored frock coat and flared tan trousers, the thin cigar that extends from his mouth offsetting a posture that leans slightly rearward, arms behind the back to broaden the shoulders.

(Interestingly enough, Spy would also depict two other figures connected to this drama. His illustration of William Gillette that appeared in February of 1907 presents the American actor in the role that gained him international recognition; I refer, of course, to the actor's stage portrayal of Sherlock Holmes. In Spy's representation, Gillette's detective, bent pipe in hand, stoops more than my friend does; but both Spy's caricature and Gillette's interpretation reflect the spirit of Holmes' intensity.

(As if not to be outdone, a few months after Gillette, Sam Clemens too served as a subject for Spy. Dressed in white but also clasping a bent pipe, Spy's bespectacled Mark Twain captures the grave demeanour that Clemens displayed to Holmes and me when tying Bates to the incriminating fingerprints. For what it's worth, Twain's pipe appears to be a calabash, which, thanks to Gillette's heralded use of it on stage, has ever since been associated with Holmes. I'm sure that Sam Clemens had smoked a calabash for years without ever giving a thought to Sherlock Holmes, but the pipe's appearance in Spy's illustration nonetheless raised questions in my mind. Had Clemens confessed to Spy his rivalry with Holmes concerning the murder on Thor Bridge? Had Spy employed the pipe as an artistic symbol representing the commonality of the two men's quests for justice?)

112

The hansom clattered past Buckingham Palace and round Hyde Park, eventually coming to a stop before the long, pale block of balconied homes known as Lancaster Gate. My friend and I climbed out of the cab and approached the black front door of No. 74, which, like its neighbours, stood between a pair of white, fluted pilasters.

Had Spy been painting the real-life version of the writer whom Holmes and I encountered that night, the acerbic humour of the caricaturist might have been too stimulated to stifle. In spite of the white hair and thick moustache the writer now sported, the Bret Harte greeting us at the door presented not the distinguished figure of an elderly patrician I was expecting, but rather the distorted image of a British clubman as aped by an aging, pock-marked denizen of the American West. The cutaway coat, striped trousers, and flowery waistcoat may have been *de rigueur* for the role; but such *accoutrements* as the *boutonnière* (in this case, a red carnation), the heavy gold watch-fob, the lavender spats, and the monocle—through which Harte was forced to squint—created a costume more appropriate for a comedic actor than for a gentleman of Mr. Harte's supposed distinction.

As mentioned earlier, I'd heard the snide rumours over the years—the gossip regarding the inhabitant of No. 74, who conveniently kept his wife of three decades back in America, whilst supposedly living with the wealthy widow of a Belgian diplomat. Certainly, no one who'd ever conversed with Sam Clemens for any length of time could fail to get an earful not only about the well-to-do widow, but also about how Harte had been sacked from his position of American Consul in Glasgow (where he'd apparently spent little time anyway); how he possessed inadequate funds to sustain himself; how his recent publications endlessly recreated an American West that existed only in their

113

author's faded memories.

If those charges weren't bad enough, it was also obvious that the man's health was weakening. From his frequent grimaces, I recognized the symptoms of facial neuralgia; and from his irregular gait and constant shuffling, I thought he must be plagued by sciatica or rheumatism or gout or lumbago. Or all of them combined. It was common knowledge that he suffered from an increasingly painful throat, and his constant effort to stifle rumblings from his stomach suggested some form of dyspepsia. And yet in spite of all these ailments, he welcomed us warmly into his rooms.

"Gentlemen, come in, come in," said he in a hoarse voice. "It is a true pleasure to meet you both. I've followed your published exploits, of course, but to entertain you in my abode—it is almost too much to wish for."

He clasped his hands together in some exaggerated expression of joy. But as he turned directly to Holmes, his demeanour grew serious; and in shaking hands with my companion, he actually pulled him closer.

"Mr. Holmes, it is to *you* I really need to speak."

My friend nodded in response, and after an awkward silence Harte turned to me. Perhaps he feared I would take offense at being neglected—though in truth I was well used to remaining in the background when Holmes was called to an investigation. Nonetheless, I appreciated the man's attempt at hospitality.

"It's most reassuring to have *you* here as well, Dr. Watson," said he. "A person in my sorry condition never knows when he might need medical help." Harte punctuated this last sentence with a stifled cough, during which his monocle fell from his eye and hung by the gold chain pinned to his lapel.

Next, he proceeded to offer us cigars—or rather *attempted* to. He couldn't locate his cigar box.

"I know it's here somewhere," he muttered, rearranging books on the various shelves that surrounded us in a vain attempt to discover the missing case. Unable to locate it among the numerous volumes, he moved to his desk, where he slid papers about on the blotter, fumbling with the brass pulls as he opened and closed various drawers. "I can't for the life of me figure out what happened to it."

"Describe the cigar box in question?" said Holmes as he scanned the room. His request may have seemed to offer aid, but I recognized it as my friend's attempt to get past this diversion and move along to the business of our meeting.

"It's made of burnished dark wood. The thing's actually a prized possession from Turkey."

"Where do you usually keep it?"

"In the top drawer of my desk, but I just looked there."

"Check again."

Harte sighed and this time dropped into the red-leather turning-chair at his desk. Grabbing hold of the pull, he opened the drawer in question about halfway, then stopped abruptly. Jerking it up and down to no avail, he cried, "It won't move any farther!"

"Allow *me*," offered Holmes. Bret Harte leaned back as my friend, sliding his long fingers into the back of the drawer, fiddled for a moment, and then withdrew the shiny wooden cigar case Harte had been seeking.

"Mr. Holmes," the writer exclaimed, "you're a genius!"

My friend offered a quick, cold smile.

Even I could perceive that the drawer had been obstructed when Harte first tried to open it—obstructed, it was now obvious, by the cigar box itself.

"Dr. Watson," the American said with a grimace that belied his happiness, "I'd like to see you create a story out of *that* little drama. I can see it now"—here he held up his hands as if framing a newspaper heading—"'The Stolen Cigar Case'."

"Not much there, I'm afraid," I chortled. "But perhaps a man of *your* talents could create a fiction about it" (which Harte would actually accomplish in 1902). "My agent, Arthur Conan Doyle, speaks most highly of your work."

Harte nodded his appreciation and, after another round of coughs, managed to say, "Let's light up together, shall we?"

In spite of the struggle to find the cigar case, Holmes and I turned down the offer. Harte, however, produced a narrow panatella. I confess that my medical instincts were aroused at the thought of a man with Harte's obvious oesophageal issues continuing to smoke.

He must have recognized my disapproval, for in response he held up the thin cigar for me to examine. "My doctor has permitted me these," said he. "They're just babies. I imagine he appreciates the fact that smoking's about the only joy I have left." Closing his eyes, he stood tall and inhaled.

"Mr. Harte," said Holmes, "can we get to the matter at hand? Let us not forget that it was *you* who summoned *me* here tonight for some professional matter. I would like to know what services of mine have caught your fancy."

Pointing his cigar at a wooden settle, our host indicated where we should sit. Thanks to the seat's straight back, Holmes and I were compelled to position ourselves severely upright. Harte, however, took the easy-chair opposite. With its deep cushions of soft-grey leather, it was clearly the most comfortable seat in the room.

Yet I couldn't quarrel with his preference. Given his

medical concerns, Harte must have hungered for every comfort available to him. Maybe seeing others seated less comfortably added to his pleasure. Indeed, he closed his eyes again as he slowly eased himself into the plush pillows. With eyes still shut, he inhaled once more; and only after a long moment did he finally let out the smoke. Apparently, Sam Clemens wasn't the only American storyteller who recognized that extending a smoke could intensify suspense.

Suddenly, Bret Harte opened his eyes. "I had a caller yesterday, Mr. Holmes," he announced, shifting in his seat to get more comfortable. "And though my physical ailments might serve to mask my anxieties, let me assure you that, appearances to the contrary, I am quite concerned."

"*The Times* mentioned such a break-in," I volunteered.

"It was not a mere break-in, Doctor," said Bret Harte. He paused dramatically for another slow intake of smoke and exhalation; then he announced: "The man came here to kill me."

I was taken aback at so singular a statement; Holmes merely nodded.

"Thomas Luck, I suspect," said Holmes, "seeking revenge."

Now it was Bret Harte's turn to look shocked. "T-Thomas Luck?" he stammered. "Revenge? After all these years? What makes you say that?"

"Elementary, Mr. Harte," said my friend. "We have been investigating a murder in Hampshire that I have reason to believe was committed by the very same Thomas Luck."

Wait a moment, I thought. *Thomas Luck may be the name written at the top of the old magazine found at Thor Place, but it's Marlow Bates who made the escape on horseback. It's Marlow Bates we suspect of murder.*

"You see, Watson," Holmes said as if reading my mind,

"now that I've witnessed Mr. Harte's reaction to the news, I am convinced that Marlow Bates is in reality one Thomas Luck."

It was my turn to stammer. "Who-who is this Thomas Luck then? And what makes you think he is also Marlow Bates?"

"Perhaps Mr. Harte can give us the background. After all, in writing 'The Luck of Roaring Camp', he introduced Thomas Luck to the world."

The writer flicked cigar ash into the Wedgewood ashtray on the cherry-wood table beside him. The smart little dish of light-blue china was charred black at the centre. "As you wish, Mr. Holmes," said Bret Harte. He closed his lips, trying to stifle some inner gases. Then he took a final pull on his panatella and carefully laid it in the ashtray.

"Many years ago in California," Harte began, "that no-account scribbler Sam Clemens and I spent some time in a cabin belonging to a friend of ours."

"Jim Gillis," I offered, thinking back to the tales I'd heard from Clemens in the Turkish baths a few months before.

Bret Harte's eyes widened. "You too are quite well informed, Doctor. I assume, then, that you also know where the cabin was located—near the silver mines in the north of the state on an incline with the distinctive name of—"

"Jackass Hill."

"Right again," said Harte.

At the same time, Holmes raised an eyebrow at me to silence my interruptions.

"Lots of people passed through that cabin—literary types in particular. On the occasion I'm talking about, though, the main attraction was a distinctive fellow named Stumpy from a mining camp—ironically or prophetically—called Hope Canyon."

"Stumpy?" I asked.

Bret Harte smiled. "In the olden days there were lots of fellows in those camps with colourful names. Why, I remember a former English sailor called 'Man-o'-War Jack'. And there was a tough from New England called 'Boston' and a fellow from somewhere in the South who called himself 'Kentuck'."

"All characters in your story," Holmes observed. "But let us not forget the woman, shall we? The one who was part Indian. You called her 'Cherokee Sal'."

"Quite so, Mr. Holmes. That was indeed her name, her *real* name. The names of all the characters were genuine; most were too colourful to pass up. But I was referring to the story-telling man who'd come to Jim Gillis' cabin. He was a short, shifty panhandler whom everyone called 'Stumpy' because of his diminutive stature."

"Clemens couldn't recall the name of the storyteller," I said. Now I wondered what else he'd forgot to mention.

"I was about to tell you," said Harte, "how the man happened to be up on Jackass Hill."

"Pray, continue," said Sherlock Holmes, crossing one long leg over the other.

Harte suppressed some more internal rumblings and went on. "It turned out that this Stumpy was on his way back from Sacramento. He'd gone there to buy clothes and such for a baby."

"A 'shifty, panhandler' named Stumpy'," said I, "doesn't sound like the type of chap to be sent shopping for baby-things."

Holmes sighed at my latest comment, yet I felt personally involved and wanted to hear the whole of the narrative with which Sam Clemens had whetted my appetite.

"You're right there, Doctor," said Harte. "But that's the beauty of the tale. You see, there happened to be a tragedy at

Hope Canyon. The baby's mother, the woman Mr. Holmes rightly identified as 'Cherokee Sal', died during the birth of her child."

"Were there no doctors in the vicinity to lend some aid?" I couldn't help asking. "One of those traveling medical men who go from camp to camp?"

"No, Doctor Watson, there was not. Not even a midwife. Sal, you see, was the only woman in the camp. But there was Stumpy. And as far as I could tell, the fact that he had two different wives off in two different places qualified him for birthing duties. Without putting too fine a point on it, he has since felt deservedly proud of his role in delivering the baby."

"But you said the poor woman died."

"Yes, Watson," Holmes ventured to explain, "but the unfortunate creature did not succumb as a result of complications from the birth itself."

"That is so," said Harte, but he had to raise a hand mid-cough to mime an apology. When his throat was clear, he added, "She suffered a gruesome, senseless death because she'd been roughed up by the man who'd fathered the baby."

"'Roughed up'?" I repeated.

Harte allowed himself a chuckle, then twisted a little in his seat and began again. "'Roughed up'. Listen to me—a respected author resorting to euphemism. In fact, pregnant as she was, she'd been gagged, beaten, stripped naked, tied to a tree, and left to die."

"Good God," I gasped.

"When they found her half-dead, Doctor, the men of Hope Canyon felt the same shock as you. Especially with the villain responsible for the tragedy conveniently gone. They knew a terrible wrong had been committed, and they wanted to set matters right. Which began with saving the baby. That's why they unanimously voted to raise the baby themselves—a boy, I might add. They agreed to feed him, educate him, clothe him—all the proper things one does in rearing a child."

"Which," Holmes put in, "included shopping for him as well—thus, explaining the mission in which Stumpy was engaged when he arrived at Jackass Hill".

"Right you are, Mr. Holmes."

"What a heart-warming story," I observed with true sincerity. "Except, of course, for the part about the poor mother. The nobility of the coarse men who saved the child is seldom appreciated. Someone should write it down."

Bret Harte smiled at my comment; but as soon as I'd said the words, I remembered what had so angered Sam Clemens: both writers had agreed *not* to repeat the tale.

"I *did* write it down," said he. "But, you see, the men wanted to keep the news of the baby as quiet as possible—despite the nobility in their actions. Rightly or wrongly, they feared that if the story got out, the local authorities would take the baby away—roughnecks like themselves could never be considered appropriate guardians for a child. So, obviously, the smaller the number of people who knew about the baby, the better."

"And yet in spite of their heartfelt fears," observed Holmes, "you took it upon yourself to publish the story anyway."

"I did," Harte proclaimed with no apparent sense of guilt. "What's more, I hoped to get it out as quickly as I could to beat Clemens to the punch. He was in the cabin at the same time, you see. He heard the narrative the same time I did, and I didn't want him publishing his version before I published mine."

"Even though he said that he wouldn't?" I countered.

Harte smiled at me again. At first, I'd thought his smile was to acknowledge the sympathy of a fellow writer; but almost immediately I recognized it as a sign of embarrassment. I could only hope that Harte realized Sam Clemens possessed an integrity that he himself did not.

"Your thinking makes perfect sense to me," said I sarcastically, my indignation growing the more the man spoke.

"And then gold was discovered," offered Holmes, directing Harte back to his narrative.

"That's right, Mr. Holmes. A couple of weeks after the child was born, the men found gold. The camp had gone so long without a strike that they figured there could be only one reason for their good fortune—the baby. What else could explain their windfall? I credited Oakhurst the gambler with the idea for the infant's last name of 'Luck'. The others added 'Thomas'"; they even held a christening. Who knows? Maybe they were thinking of the Apostle."

Thomas Luck—most memorable. Still, the fact that Luck had changed his name to "Marlow Bates" didn't make him a murderer. The miners had wanted to keep the story quiet; perhaps Thomas Luck had sought a new name to conceal his relationship to Harte's story. *Fame isn't craved by everyone, Bret Harte notwithstanding.*

"One must assume," I prodded, "that with their newfound good fortune, the miners had even more cause to conceal the story. They didn't want to risk losing their talisman."

"Exactly, Doctor. They presumed the child would continue to bring them more gold."

"Then why would this Stumpy speak so freely in front of strangers?" I asked.

Bret Harte paused to replace the monocle in his right eye whilst squinting with his left and staring at both of us like a lopsided Cyclops. "Stumpy wasn't worried. He was well

acquainted with all three Gillis brothers—Jim, Steve, and Billy—
and knew he could trust each of them. No doubt he believed he
could trust their friends as well—if he even paid us any mind."
Now Harte trained his single lens on me. "As a writer yourself,
Doctor, I'm sure you'll agree that once this Stumpy started talking,
it was my good luck that he forgot Clemens and I were even
there."

However ignoble Harte's point, I could understand his
attitude. But Holmes didn't give me the opportunity to respond.
He spoke in a voice tinged with anger: "I can only assume, Mr.
Harte, that once the storyteller realized that two complete
strangers, two eavesdropping writers, had, in fact, heard his story,
that was when he asked you both—even if you *were* friends of the
Gillises—not to tell the facts to anyone, let alone write them
down. Is that not correct?"

"To be entirely accurate," Harte said, stifling another
cough, "he never said anything about not *writing* the story—
though he did ask us not to *tell* it. Actually, he *begged* us not to tell
it—first, in the name of the baby and all his comrades and then in
the name of the child's murdered mother. But—" (here he
directed his monocled stare at me again) "—an experienced
writer can recognize a tale that's too good to pass up. I'm sure, Dr.
Watson, that you intuitively sense which of your investigations
with Sherlock Holmes make the best reading and are, therefore,
the best ones to transcribe. *My* readers like sentimental sketches.
And this one about a group of seasoned miners raising a baby
from birth? Well, I couldn't ignore it. In fact, it was to emphasize
the infant's name that I called the story 'The Luck of Roaring
Camp'."

Sherlock Holmes pointed his long forefinger at Bret Harte.
"You, Mr. Harte—unlike Samuel Clemens—wrote and published

that story without anyone's permission. In fact, you wrote it in the face of pleas to the contrary. It first appeared in the August '68 edition of *The Overland Monthly*, the magazine that you yourself edited."

Bret Harte smiled sheepishly. "Guilty, Mr. Holmes. But at least give me credit for disguising some of the identifying features. I may have kept people's real names, but I did set the story some ten years earlier and change the location from Hope Canyon to Roaring Camp. And I never mentioned that Sal had been constrained and beaten. What is most important, however, is that in *my* version of the history, the baby dies. I drowned Tommy Luck in a flood when he was still an infant. I made the North Fork River overflow, and I killed him and his protector, the man named Kentuck."

"You sound like God," I said quietly.

Bret Harte removed the monocle from his eye and began fidgeting with the lens.

"I don't understand," said I. "If the fictional baby was killed and the true locations weren't named, no one would have any reason to go looking for the source of your story. They wouldn't know where to start."

"My thoughts exactly, sir," said Harte enthusiastically. "My thoughts exactly." He shook his monocle at me for confirmation, but his excitement led to a crescendo of coughs.

I still didn't understand. "So why is Thomas Luck so angry that he's threatened to kill you? He was just a baby when this Stumpy asked you not to repeat the story."

"I don't know. But angry he is; and the reason I contacted you, Mr. Holmes, is because he's angry with you as well, and he wanted me to tell you so."

"Really!" said Holmes, doing nothing to conceal a self-satisfied smile. I knew how much he appreciated receiving compliments from even the vilest of miscreants—*especially* by the vilest of miscreants.

"Yes. As far as I can see, Mr. Holmes, Thomas Luck blames *you* for causing all his troubles. He claimed you proved that some woman's suicide was *not* a suicide—whatever that means. He had some rude comments to make about Sam Clemens as well." A quick grin blossomed in Harte's troubled face. "Of course, I had to agree with him about that low-life."

I ignored this last comment, concerned instead with Harte's reference to Maria Gibson's false suicide. "There's an additional puzzle, Holmes," said I, "the connection between Thomas Luck and Gibson's wife. Why would he want to kill *her*?"

Sherlock Holmes leaned as far back as the settee would allow, putting his fingers together to form a steeple. He reflected for a moment and then said, "Think carefully, Mr. Harte. Could somebody else besides you, Clemens, and the Gillis brothers have heard this story? Was there anyone else in the cabin when Stumpy reported the facts?"

Harte slowly shook his head. "You're asking me to remember the peripheries of something that happened forty years ago," said he, readjusting the cushions of his chair. Despite the softness of the leather, at each movement he clenched his teeth to absorb the pain.

"It's possible there were others there," he continued. "It's hard to say. It was a large cabin and quite dark. And remember that I was concentrating on every last detail of the story being told. I only recall Sam Clemens so vividly because that was the only time the two of us had ever travelled up there together. But just I already told you, lots of people found their way to Jackass Hill."

He paused, seemingly to reflect some more on the topic. At the same time, he removed a linen handkerchief from an inside breast pocket and employed it to wipe clean both sides of his monocle. Finally, he said, "No, I can't recall anyone else."

"If Thomas Luck was so angry with you, Mr. Harte," I asked, "why didn't he harm you when he was here? Why do you think he left you alone?"

The American writer smiled wanly. "That's easy. He took one look at me—saw the pain in my movements, listened to my voice—and rightly concluded that I'm dying. 'Let the Lord finish you off,' he said." The writer took another pull on his cigar and stared off at nothing in particular.

We thanked Bret Harte for his information. Needless to say, we would have to notify Sam Clemens of these developments. If Thomas Luck sought vengeance against Sherlock Holmes for revealing the staged suicide, it only followed that Luck would harbour equally murderous thoughts towards the man who'd actually identified Luck as the killer.

"Should Thomas Luck return to America," said Holmes, "Clemens could be in grave danger. Should Luck remain in England, Watson, his desire for revenge might very well lead him to Baker Street."

Chapter Ten

An enemy can partly ruin a man,
but it takes a good-natured injudicious friend
to complete the thing and make it perfect.
--Mark Twain
Pudd'nhead Wilson

In spite of all the talk of vengeance, we heard nothing more of Thomas Luck following his encounter with Bret Harte. I did send a letter to Clemens warning him of the danger he might be in on the heels of the threat to Harte, but all I received in return was a brief lament about Luck's having failed to kill the "son of a bitch" when he'd had the chance. Wherever Thomas Luck had gone, it was to a most successful hideaway. Indeed, for all we knew, the villain might have died. Or fallen off of the planet—at least, off of England's share of it. Though we couldn't predict it at the time, of course, Luck's absence would last seven years.

Regardless of the duration, Sherlock Holmes remained on the alert. But then, as I've already mentioned, he was always at the ready. "Watson," he'd cautioned, "in my line of work, one has to be vigilant all the time."

Though Luck might have vanished, as a result of the evidence turned up in our enquiry, the murder he'd committed in Hampshire continued to occupy central stage for many months. At least, it did in *my* mind. For I still believed that the deductive skills Holmes revealed in the investigation deserved to be made public. After all, the master detective had been at the top of his game when he deduced from the chip above the bridge's balustrade how the murder weapon had been made to disappear in order to cast blame on the governess.

So clever did I think the inferences of my friend that I maintained they overshadowed the two facts of the investigation that bothered me the most: one, that Bates (or Luck), the true murderer, had escaped; and, two, that it was Sam Clemens, not Holmes, who had produced the fingerprints which ultimately revealed the identity of the culprit. In spite of these challenges, I still wanted to publish my account of the case, the narrative which by then I had come to title "The Problem of Thor Bridge". I reasoned that whilst highlighting Holmes' brilliant deductions, I could easily minimize Bates' disappearance as well as Clemens' fingerprint-evidence.

It was my literary agent who warned me to avoid such problematic developments entirely. Conan Doyle called them "fatal fractures in the foundation of your hero," the trilled "r's" in his Scottish accent giving added certitude to his pronouncements.

In spite of Conan Doyle's strength of conviction, however, I persisted in disagreeing, and thus was born the portentous difference of opinions I described at the start of this narrative, the difference of opinions that would ignite Clemens' rage.

To exchange more fully our ideas on the role of Samuel Clemens and the matter of Thor Bridge, Conan Doyle and I met for dinner at Simpson's. From the start I couldn't fathom his argument. He maintained that the slightest mention of Clemens' insights would only serve to highlight Holmes' deficiencies. I reminded him that no other cases in which I'd reported Holmes' shortcomings had ever troubled him before.

Such setbacks certainly hadn't troubled Sherlock Holmes.

He actually encouraged me to report his infrequent blunders.

"Watson, old fellow," he'd said in various ways on more than one occasion, "whenever I seem overconfident in my powers or giving less attention to a case than it deserves, be sure to remind me of my missteps."

Readers need only recall the oversights I recorded in any number of Holmes' exploits to confirm that I fulfilled his request. Irene Adler's triumph comes to mind in the story I titled "A Scandal in Bohemia". There was also the over-extended search for the stolen racehorse Silver Blaze and the dangerous pursuit of the missing Lady Frances Carfax and the profound misidentification of the so-called "yellow face". Sherlock Holmes didn't always get it right, and in none of my accounts of these cases did Conan Doyle voice an iota of criticism.

For some reason, however, in the matter of Thor Bridge, the man would not be placated. Perhaps his recent wartime medical experiences in Bloemfontein had made him more cautious—or more appreciative of the public's need for heroes.

"You don't want your readers to discover that Holmes has feet of clay," he cautioned, pausing only long enough to order a cut of beef from one of Simpson's silver-domed trolleys. "Holmes' mental acuity is his strength." He pointed his fork in my direction for emphasis as he warned, "Do not allow his power to spear diminished—as you surely would by revealing his dependency on Clemens. And it should go without saying that you certainly don't want to alarm the public with the news that the murderer, this Thomas Luck—or is it Marlow Bates?—remains at large."

In a word, Conan Doyle urged me to revise the story. He wanted me to omit not only the role of Sam Clemens but also that of Thomas Luck and—instead of announcing an unsolved murder—to conclude the plot with the revelation of Mrs. Gibson's suicide. Such editing, he allowed, would enable me to highlight the skills of my protagonist without raising the issue of Holmes' miscalculations or calling attention to the murderer's escape.

"And whilst you're revising," he concluded with a wink, "begin the piece with some righteous diversion about your philosophy of composition. Trust me. Confess that you're withholding facts whose revelation might cause consternation to innocent parties, and you'll gain nothing but sympathy from your readers."

In fairness to the man, Conan Doyle had come to my aid before, especially on matters American in *A Study in Scarlet* and *The Valley of Fear*. One could also not deny that he understood the marketplace. In one singular example, the grand success of his novel *The White Company* rendered foolish any attempt of my part to ignore his advice. And I didn't; I accepted his recommendations.

I'm not proud of my actions. Even though key figures in the drama—like Marlow Bates, whom I never identified as "Thomas Luck" in my original version, and The Gold King, Senator Gibson—would appear much more benign than they were in reality, I acquiesced. As for Sam Clemens, he wouldn't appear at all.

Though I completed "The Problem of Thor Bridge" according to Conan Doyle's insightful suggestions, the exclusion of Clemens from the account continued to trouble me. In fact, so guilt-ridden did I feel that early in 1901, well before I intended the story to be published, I sent the galley proofs to America so Clemens himself could peruse the text before it appeared in public. Early receipt of the story, I reasoned, would cushion the shock. At the very least, he would be ahead of my readers in discovering that, in spite of being the sleuth who'd identified the murderer, Samuel L. Clemens did not appear at all in my report of the investigation.

In truth, I must have been hoping for some sort of approval or permission from the man. Looking back on it now, however, I can only laugh at my foolish expectations. As a person who'd spent not an insignificant amount of time with Clemens, I should have known that anyone as self-centred as he would never tolerate his own exclusion from a story. He himself had hinted as much. At some point, Clemens told me that when his daughter Suzy was thirteen, she'd written of her father, "When Papa was at home, there wasn't enough air for the rest of us." Obviously, she had more insight into the man than I ever did.

At the same time, I must also confess that with the events in the world dominating my thoughts, I allowed my literary concerns to slip further into the background. For many months, the failing health of Queen Victoria had been a cause for worry throughout the Empire; yet when the actual death of Her Majesty occurred in late January of 1901, the tragic news still shocked us all. Most people then alive had grown up knowing no other monarch, and the national mourning for the Queen and the subsequent ascension of her son Edward VII preoccupied all of England—if not the entire globe. Additional bad news reached our shores from America only a few months later with word of President McKinley's assassination. A deranged anarchist named Leon Czolgosz had shot the President at the Pan-American Exposition in Buffalo, New York.

In the midst of such dark tidings, I trust that charitable readers will forgive me for taking little notice that a year had slipped by and I had received from Sam Clemens not a word—let alone any hint of displeasure—regarding the galley proofs I'd sent him of "The Problem of Thor Bridge". Furthermore, that letter to

Joe Twichell revealing Clemens' resentment of Holmes wouldn't be made public for years. With no reason to anticipate Clemens' hostility, therefore, I adopted the adage that "no news is good news" and put the entire controversy out of mind.

I should have known better.

***

Evidence of Clemens' rage didn't arrive at Baker Street until April of '02. Even then it didn't appear in the form of some angry letter like the missive to Twichell, but rather in a benign parcel addressed to Sherlock Holmes. Delivered by post, wrapped in brown paper, and secured with twine, it contained the red-covered, single-volume copy of Mark Twain's "A Double-Barrelled Detective Story" that caused the devastation with which I began this account. Dripping with sarcasm, an accompanying note read, *"Sorry I couldn't send the proofs, but I thought an early copy of a bound first edition might please you."* It was signed, *"SC"*.

Truth be told, I'd heard rumours as early as January of a spoof about Holmes appearing in an American magazine, but even today one can't go searching for each and every piece of writing about my friend that pops up. The number is endless. After all, images of successful people command the attention of the public—often, I'm sad to say, the *envy* of the public—and it is often the most sombre of such successes, figures like Sherlock Holmes, that attract the most criticism and derision.

Even more disheartening were the belittling words of people who'd actually met the man—not just read my accounts—and still considered him a fair target for ridicule. Bret Harte serves as an example. In less than two months following our visit to Lancaster Gate, he published the comical story to which I alluded earlier, "The Stolen Cigar-Case". Appearing in *Pearson's Magazine*, it presented a detective named Hemlock Jones, who attempts to solve the very mystery about which Harte and I had bantered the evening of our meeting: the location of the missing cigar box. Unlike reality, however, Jones believes a robbery has been committed; and his primary suspect is the medical man who is reporting the story. I should laugh! Any implied similarity between the fawning narrator and myself exposes Harte's reliance on hyperbole.

Holmes himself saw no humour in Harte's story, but I could not stop sniggering. It seemed clear to me that however much Bret Hart had been ailing in his later years, he still could produce entertaining fiction. In truth, thanks to his witty prose, I could understand why Conan Doyle spoke so highly of the man's literary talents. Anyone could tell that Harte had intended his cigar-case story as a burlesque and—unlike Clemens' bitter tale, which was published later—not to be taken seriously. Despite the eerie similarity of the detectives' names—Harte's Hemlock Jones and Clemens' Fetlock Jones—the stark contrast in tone between the two narratives makes one wonder if by so ruthlessly denigrating Holmes, Clemens was simply seeking to show he could stoop lower than his long-time American rival.

That Bret Harte's parody of Holmes was light-hearted is not to deify the author. His ethics, about which we'd already heard from Sam Clemens, were another matter. Harte's duplicitous nature went beyond writing a story he'd pledged not to divulge or living with a woman to whom he was not legally married. When Harte died in May of '02, he left no inheritance to his wife or daughter, the two of them then in England. Conan Doyle was one of a number of public figures that raised money for the pair, and soon enough Bret Harte's daughter would actually open a typewriting bureau in Baker Street just down the road from 221.

But I digress. As the recorder of the exploits of Sherlock Holmes, I claim no great insights into the writing of humour. It is a foreign land within whose bourn I have had little cause to travel. And yet my sensibilities tell me that sketches like "A Double-Barrelled Detective Story", which on the surface seek to entertain through ludicrous comedy—how else to account for a character named Ham Sandwich?—should not also go about depicting the humiliation of a pregnant woman.

If, however, one assumes that the true target of Clemens' satire was not fictional crimes stories in general but the very real Mr. Sherlock Holmes, then Clemens' references to the murderous events in Hampshire make more sense. Why else would Clemens call the mining camp in his story where the fictional Holmes is belittled "Hope Canyon", the same ironical name as the true location of Cherokee Sal's death? Why else identify the date of the amateur sleuth's arrival in Hope Canyon as 3 October 1900, the very same day that Senator Gibson had sent his note to Baker Street that set into motion the investigation of the murder at Thor Bridge? Why else include a character whose alias, "David Wilson", employs Pudd'nhead Wilson's rightful forename, if not to evoke Mark Twain's eponymous novel in which the title-character masters the science of analysing fingerprints? Sam Clemens offered clues destined to enhance the force of his insidious attack on Holmes at the same time he was holding up to ridicule the analytical methods of the world's first consulting detective.

As the solitary hero of my censored account of events at Thor Place, it was Sherlock Holmes who served as Clemens' target—not I, its author. As a consequence, it was my friend who suffered severe melancholy following the publication of Clemens' malicious story. Particularly troubling in the early summer of '02 was Holmes' avoidance of social interaction. I remember the period quite clearly as it presaged that memorable investigation of the three Garridebs during which I suffered the misfortune of being shot. Before involving himself in that case, however, Holmes spent full days sleeping in the gloomy confines of his curtained room. Though I've never expressed the opinion before, I believe that he took on the additional work in those next few months to insulate himself from the effects of Clemens' literary assault.

Worse still, investigations weren't all that Holmes ignored. He expressed no interest in attending the upcoming coronation of King Edward, and he made it abundantly clear that he would refuse the knighthood about to be offered him for services previously rendered. (Fortunately, Holmes' obstinacy did not infect Conan Doyle, whose own knighthood was announced as part of the coronation ceremonies in August.) So concerned did I grow about my friend's well being that I found myself longing for the reassuring wails of his violin. I never saw the poor man resort to his needle during this dark period, but one can imagine the psychological damage he suffered. And this depression lasted many months.

In fairness, I should also report that I too suffered during this period. Even though it had been Conan Doyle's suggestion and not my own to omit Clemens from the narrative, I couldn't forget that I was the one who had enacted the insensitive recommendations. I was the one who had prompted Clemens' attack on my friend, and that fact made me feel ultimately responsible for Holmes' emotional distress.

One needn't be a literary scholar—or a psychologist, for that matter—to recognize the expression of discomfort in the ambiguous wording of my title, "The Problem of Thor Bridge". The narrative remains my only account of Holmes' exploits with the word "problem" in the title. I thought it clever at the time; but in retrospect, it seems obvious that the story's name refers not only to the criminal "problem" of finding the identity of Mrs. Gibson's killer, but also to my personal "problem" of having promulgated Conan Doyle's adulterated version of the truth. I feel certain that it was this dissatisfaction with the expurgated narrative—not to mention my desire to avoid increasing Holmes' misery by publishing it—that caused me to hide away the original manuscript for more than twenty years.

Thankfully, as the months lumbered past, Holmes grew stronger. By July he was feeling confident enough to leave England for Switzerland on the trail of the Lady Frances Carfax, and the dramatic success of that case seemed to restore his old self. The crisis had passed.

As for Clemens, one could always hope that in constructing his attack on Holmes, he had rid himself of whatever dark feelings my truncated narrative had generated. Free of such demons, the ever-busy writer might now turn to a more tranquil and serene existence. The autobiography he was reportedly writing could surely offer him new opportunities for reflection and appreciation.

Life, however, is never so simple. Even if composing his vitriolic story did serve as a catharsis for the man, such an emotional release could do nothing to spare Clemens from the subsequent traumas that came to preoccupy his life. His beloved Livy grew ill some six months after the appearance of her husband's vicious tale, and the two of them would move to Italy in hopes of encountering a restorative locale. But Mrs. Clemens' constitution continued to decline, and the dear woman, whom I'd been honoured to meet at Dollis Hill House four years earlier, died in Florence in 1904.

Samuel Clemens was never the same. He'd lost his daughter Suzy not that long before and now he'd lost Livy. He would soon find himself institutionalizing his epileptic daughter Jean and ultimately watching her die as well. No one can doubt that in his latter years, life had dealt the man a demoralizing hand. And whilst I had nothing to do with these particular calamities, I'll never rid myself of the fear that the galley proofs, which I had foolishly sent to Sam Clemens, contributed to his continuing malaise.

And yet in the face of all his personal tragedies, Sam Clemens soldiered on. He travelled the lecture circuit and publicly celebrated his seventieth-birthday at the famous Delmonico's Restaurant in New York. In Connecticut, he built a new home called Stormfield. But the pleasures he experienced were hardly sufficient to interrupt the continuous flow of bitter pieces he's reputed to have penned in those years—works so dark about the hollowness, the emptiness, the sadness, which he'd come to associate with human existence, that he prohibited them from being published until fifty years after his death.

Lest I be accused of distorting the truth yet again, however, I must not leave the impression that curse-like misfortune dogged all the major personages related to the matter of Thor Bridge. Some positive happenings did indeed occur in the period following our investigation.

In late 1901 at a small ceremony in the city of Winchester, Senator Jedidiah Gibson married Grace Dunbar. Not long thereafter, in a story that belongs in some other volume, I too took a bride, exchanging my old address for a house near Harley Street, the province of numerous physicians. In the fall of '03, Sherlock

Holmes also vacated our old rooms and, much to the consternation of Mrs. Hudson, established himself in a cottage on the Sussex Downs. In that picturesque locale, Holmes hoped to initiate his long-time plan not only of creating and maintaining a colony of bees, but also of writing a monograph on their behaviour. More than once he'd said to me, "Watson, it is the segregation of the queen that fascinates me most."

For a number of us then, the new century appeared to begin on a note of optimism. And yet "The Problem of Thor Bridge" constantly nagged. Although I continued to regard the manuscript as one of my best recreations of Holmes' intellectual powers, for two decades I allowed it to moulder in my dispatch box in the vaults of Cox and Co. of Charing Cross. In early 1922, I could bear it no longer. Still steadfastly wed to the concept that the reading public deserved every opportunity to witness my friend's talent in the pursuit of justice, I finally permitted the censored story to appear in *The Strand* and in *Hearst's International.*

Chapter Eleven

All kings is mostly rapscallions.
--Mark Twain
Huckleberry Finn

During the almost seven years following our investigation of the events on Thor Bridge, Sherlock Holmes and I encountered each other on only rare occasions. Whenever we did, of course—at his cottage in Sussex, at my home in London, or at some nostalgic restaurant in Covent Garden or in the Strand—we always found familiar topics to discuss. Our conversations usually centred on past cases; yet in spite of the many investigations we reviewed, there was always one we managed to avoid. Holmes and I never talked about the unsatisfying end to our enquiry concerning that fateful night on the bridge in Hampshire.

Our lingering silence on the subject demonstrated a maxim that veteran investigators consistently maintain: no matter how much one ignores unresolved cases, they never disappear. The murder of Maria Gibson presented just such a dilemma. I knew that I had never let it go; what's more, I felt certain that neither had Holmes. Oh, there may have been no recent news concerning the whereabouts of Thomas Luck; but I suspected that, retired or not, somewhere in the back of his mind, Sherlock Holmes was keeping open a file on the fugitive. If the slightest hint of the man appeared in a newspaper or magazine, I had no doubt that Holmes would discover it.

No matter how much I tried to ignore the case, however, a news report in May of 1907 revealed to me just how close to the surface were my own memories of the murder. An article in the *Times* announced that Samuel Langhorne Clemens, having been invited to receive an honorary degree in literature from Oxford, would be sailing to England the next month. Years before, I had read that upon his last return to the States, Clemens had vowed he would never cross the Atlantic again; but at the risk of contradicting himself, he proclaimed that to procure a degree from Oxford, he "would be willing to journey to Mars".

Remembering the man's high opinion of himself, I had to laugh. No doubt, he believed that such an honour merely confirmed his own view of the lofty position he felt destined to occupy in the literary firmament. At the same time, one couldn't disagree with the estimation; countless thousands would welcome the triumphant return of the American to English soil. Yet for me, the snippet of news was enough to waft back into my consciousness the sour smell of Maria Gibson's murder and its bitter aftermath.

In spite of his retirement, I assumed that Sherlock Holmes had also heard of Clemens' impending visit. Still, I had to be certain. I wanted to protect my friend from being taken by surprise. I knew that Holmes would never forgive Sam Clemens for the humiliating story Clemens had written, and the sooner I informed Holmes of the writer's plans the better. Besides, conveying the news myself offered me a reason for visiting the Sussex Downs, always a pleasant journey but especially so in the spring; and thus I travelled south to Holmes' cottage early one morning at the start of June.

By now the route was familiar to me: The rails take one over verdant hills, past the red and yellow and purple hues of wildflowers, through the sunlight-perforated forests, and finally down to the chalky white cliffs overlooking the Channel. In the train station at the seaside city of Eastbourne some five miles from Holmes' cottage, I boarded an omnibus, and in the nearby village of Fulworth I hired a dogcart to take me the remaining distance to my friend's retreat.

I had hoped to offer Holmes the information about the return of Sam Clemens as soon as I arrived, but it had slipped my mind that the ageless Mrs. Hudson had moved to the South Downs to serve as Holmes' housekeeper.

"Dr. Watson," she greeted me, eyes twinkling. "Preparing breakfast for the two of you gentlemen will be just like old times."

One look at the late-morning presentation of kippers, tomatoes, eggs and rashers she'd set out in the small dining room, and I realized the need to maintain an amiable atmosphere. There was no point in ruining Mrs. Hudson's excellent meal with so distasteful a topic for Holmes as news about Samuel Clemens.

Only when we were drinking our coffees, did I get round to telling him of the Oxford degree that Clemens was coming to claim.

"Mmmmm," Sherlock Holmes intoned staring into the dark brew, "nothing of real importance going on in the world then."

I had no idea if Holmes had already heard the report, but we spoke no more of the matter. The entire country may have been agog in anticipation of Sam Clemens' visit, but Sherlock Holmes seemed content to sit silently nursing a cup of coffee at his breakfast table on the South Downs.

* * *

It required less than a fortnight following my journey to Holmes' cottage for London to turn topsy-turvy over the arrival of Samuel Clemens. Like the onrushing tides that overwhelm the sandy shores, crowds numbering in the thousands invaded Mayfair on an overcast Tuesday morning, the eighteenth of June. Gathering round Brown's Hotel in Albermarle Street, they hoped to welcome the American author personally.

The early papers reported that Clemens' ship, the Atlantic Transport Liner *Minneapolis,* enveloped by the earthy smell of the cattle it was also transporting, had put in at the Tilbury docks at 4:00 in the morning. Following breakfast, the writer would be setting off for his hotel. Celebrated raconteur that he was, however, the sun-tanned and bespectacled author, clad in black bowler, white tie, and lounge suit of dove-grey with matching overcoat, found himself unable to walk past the group of pressmen waiting for him on the deck. He bit off the end of a long black cigar, lit up, and, leaning against the iron bulwarks of the *Minneapolis,* delivered his pronouncements to a devoted audience that took down his observations as if Clemens' words had come from heaven itself.

It would be easy to insert the countless witticisms and *bon mots* of Mark Twain that have been roundly recorded by these self-same newspapermen who followed him everywhere during the trip: how, for instance, with a twinkle in his eye he announced that in receiving his Oxford honours, he would show the English what a *real* American college boy looked like; how with his umbrella raised, he told everyone that the brolly was made of cotton—the only kind an Englishman wouldn't steal; how with the Doctor of Letters degree in his immediate future, he could admit that such an honour would make him a multi-millionaire—if only he could turn what he didn't know about letters into cash.

The purpose of this narrative, however, is to correct the historical record concerning a literary artist's role in solving a violent crime and not to sing the praises of the man's acerbic wit—however deserving such praise might be. More comedic-minded scribblers than I may illustrate the considerable talents of Sam Clemens; I will continue to focus my attention on the events surrounding the terrible murder on Thor Bridge that had taken place almost seven years before.

When his shipboard colloquy with the pressmen finally broke up, Clemens manoeuvred down the gangway in the company of his secretary, Ralph Ashcroft. Clemens called his traveling aide a "professional nurse." Ashcroft was a bearded young man, who center-parted his dark hair, sported a well-tailored blue suit, and hailed from Liverpool.

Upon reaching the foot of the gangway, the distinctive writer with the wayward white hair was instantly recognized. According to the reports, no sooner did he set foot on the dock than cheers of welcome erupted from longshoremen working nearby. Clemens acknowledged them all with a spirited wave; and then, along with Ashcroft and the other passengers from the *Minneapolis*, made his way to the boat train that would convey him to St. Pancras Station where, at that same instant, ever larger and more clamorous crowds were gathering.

The sudden increase in the local population, however, was less of a surprise to me than the wire I received from Sherlock Holmes later that same day. Usually our exchanges took the form of letters. A wire carries with it a sense of urgency; and my concern was only strengthened by Holmes' request that, upon hearing no word to the contrary, he be allowed to call on me the following afternoon. Save for the occasional concert at the Albert

Hall, Holmes rarely came up to London anymore; and given the large crowds attendant on Clemens' every move, I could only conclude that some matter of great importance had to be compelling him to brave the throngs in the city.

My inferences turned out to be correct. Directly after lunch on Wednesday, Holmes arrived at our front door with Gladstone in hand. He was a little greyer than I remembered him, but then so was I.

"Of course, old fellow," I answered when he asked if the spare room, our so-called bachelor quarters, was still available for a few nights' stay. "You're more than welcome."

My wife greeted Holmes warmly and then left the two of us on our own to talk about whatever it was that had brought him to London. She recognized our need for privacy and had made arrangements to visit a friend.

Sherlock Holmes joined me in the sitting room, but waved away my offers of tea and tobacco as we seated ourselves on either side of the red-mahogany butler's table. He took the antimacassared blue-silk chair; I, the leather wing chair opposite.

"Jedidiah Gibson came to see me yesterday, Watson," Holmes startled me by announcing.

"Senator Gibson?" It was a name we hadn't discussed in years. "At your cottage?"

"Yes. For the record, he motored over from Thor Place in a Rolls Royce Silver Ghost. By the by, I think that the new Mrs. Gibson—that is, the former Grace Dunbar—has had a most calming effect on the man."

A *relative term, "The* new *Mrs. Gibson"*, I couldn't help thinking. After all, she and the Senator had now been married for more than five years.

"Gibson said that he had an urgent matter to discuss with

me, but he first wanted was to apologize for upsetting my retirement."

I leaned forward attentively.

"He showed me this note, Watson. It'd come to him through the post."

Careful to grasp it by its edges, Holmes removed a small piece of light-blue writing paper from an inside pocket and held it up before me. I reached out to take it, but Holmes shook his head. He wanted as few people handling it as possible. Even without touching the page, I could easily discern a brief, handwritten message in large, black, cursive script: *"When you strike at a king, you must kill him."*

"What does this mean, Holmes?"

"It's a quotation from Ralph Waldo Emerson, the American philosopher."

Despite the threat of violence in the note, I was impressed that Holmes had recognized the source. "Since when have you taken an interest in philosophy?" It was another of those liberal arts I'd initially labelled Holmes' knowledge of as "nil".

"I regard Emerson as a dispenser of pragmatic wisdom," said he as placed the note on the butler's table, "not as some abstract thinker. 'Know thyself,' he advised; 'learn from nature.' Good lessons to be sure, and very practical indeed."

I knew there had to be a point to all this, and I asked again, "The note—what does it mean? Who sent it?"

"I believe it to be a veiled threat."

"Against whom?"

"Really, Watson? I thought that would be obvious from the quotation. Does it not mention striking a king?"

I looked at him in disbelief. "Surely you can't mean His Royal Highness?"

"That might be the usual assumption," said Holmes with the smile he employed with an explanation quick at hand. "But you seem to be forgetting the Senator's sobriquet."

"Ah, yes—'the Gold King'."

"Someone else has obviously *not* forgot it. Who? Who might have sent such a threat?"

"Obviously, you have someone in mind, Holmes. Who indeed?"

"It required no great feat of detection to answer that question, old fellow. Gibson immediately recognized the handwriting. It took him only a moment to resurrect a familiar villain, Marlow Bates—that is, Thomas Luck."

"Thomas Luck?" I cried, transfixed by the evocation of a name neither one of us had uttered in close to seven years. "Look here," I said, pointing to the note lying before us. It's unsigned. How can you be sure it was Luck who sent it?"

Holmes smiled again. "Recall that Luck was the manager of Gibson's estate, Watson. The Senator is more than familiar with Luck's penmanship. In fact, since Luck could anticipate no less from the Senator and still did nothing to alter his script, it 's obvious that Luck made no effort to conceal his identity."

Holmes picked up the note at its edges and held it before me. "The paper itself is of ordinary stock that can be purchased almost anywhere. So is the Indian ink. The envelope was postmarked at Stow-on-the-Wold."

"The Cotswolds, then?"

"Yes, Watson. What's more, the note contains finger-marks. Even better, you'll be happy to learn that I was not too vain to keep the prints that Clemens had so cleverly secured from Luck. After Luck had fled Thor Place, I retrieved the glass Clemens had taken from him, dusted some black powder onto the oil left by Luck's fingers, and then carefully lifted the prints from the surface with the aid of an adhesive tape. I've maintained those prints in my files ever since. Just yesterday I compared them to those I found on the note to the Senator. Gibson's were there as well, of course, but I most certainly found Luck's."

"And you say the envelope was postmarked in Stow?"

"Think of it, Watson. What better place in which to get lost than the Cotswolds? Stow is on a main road with access to all parts of the country, and work is plentiful. Many a farm might be looking for random help—perhaps he signed on somewhere as a shepherd or farmer of sorts. He served as Gibson's estates manager, let us not forget. For that matter, he must have studied accounting or bookkeeping to qualify for his position with Gibson. With such a background, he might have got a job in Stow itself or in any of the other towns nearby—there are so many, after all."

I was dumbfounded. It had been so many years. "Why *now*, Holmes?" I asked. "What do you think has awakened Thomas Luck?"

"Two good questions, Watson," said Holmes, returning the note to the table. "I have my suspicions, though I am not yet prepared to offer answers. Even without identifying the specific catalyst, however, we must assume that the cold-blooded murderer of Mrs. Gibson is once more on the prowl."

"To hear you put it that way, Holmes, I must ask about the precautions Gibson has taken to protect himself."

Holmes nodded. "Another good question, old fellow, one which I *am* able to answer. I told Senator Gibson to notify Sergeant Coventry—who, by the by, is now an inspector. Coventry wired Scotland Yard for reinforcement; and though the Met are overwhelmed by the crowds here in London, they nonetheless have managed to send a few men down to Hampshire."

"Good. Gaining protection for Gibson seems the appropriate response. And yet your behaviour makes me wonder. In spite of your worries about his safety, you didn't go to Thor Place yourself; instead, you've come all the way to London. What else bothers you about this affair."

"Ah, Watson," Holmes sighed. "How well you read my troubled mind. I admit to sharing your initial fear—concerning His Majesty. I can't believe that Luck would have any reason to attack King Edward. But it is possible that I could be wrong about Gibson. What if Luck wants us to think that his target is the Senator when, in fact, killing His Royal Highness may be the true goal of this madman? It is too great a risk to discount. Ignoring His Majesty would be a miscalculation of the greatest order."

"But certainly a man like Luck could never get close to the King."

"On the contrary, Watson. The King is hosting a garden party for the Oxford degree recipients on Saturday at Windsor. Thousands of guests will be milling about. It provides a perfect opportunity for mayhem."

"Good God," I said, "today is already Thursday."

"That's why I went directly to Scotland Yard before coming here. I informed our old friend, Chief Inspector Stanley Hopkins, of my concerns."

"*Chief* Inspector is it now?"

"*Tempus fugit*, old fellow. It's been more than ten years since our first case with the man. He's past forty."

Now I wasn't surprised that Stanley Hopkins had climbed the ranks. He'd been a promising detective with quite the eye for uncovering evidence. What's more, he had always been one of the few officials who appreciated my friend's work. I still recall the policeman's cries of "Wonderful! Wonderful!" that greeted

Holmes' revelations, and my friend quite obviously relished Hopkins' characterization of Holmes as "master" and himself as "pupil".

Yet from the start Holmes harboured reservations about the man's judgement, about his nagging inability to understand the import of what he'd uncovered. The detective's arrest of the wrong man in the "Black Peter" investigation and his inability to piece together the evidence of the murder at the Abbey Grange in Kent serve as two examples.

"I told Hopkins," said Holmes, "that you and I would meet him at Windsor Castle tomorrow evening—assuming, of course, there's no attack upon the Gold King here in Hampshire before then. Also assuming that you're available to join me."

"Why, Holmes, how can you even ask? The nation's honour is at stake. My locum will look after my surgery, and Mrs. Watson is more than understanding.

Again I asked, "But why do you think this is happening now? Of all people, why would Bates suddenly take it into his head to kill the King?"

"I don't know, Watson. Perhaps the return to England of Samuel Clemens has re-ignited some long dormant rage inside the man."

* * *

In the next two days, the police assigned to Thor Place detected no suspicious activities. While such news was welcoming to Senator Gibson, it caused Holmes and me to focus our concerns more directly on the well being of King Edward and his upcoming garden party. To that end, under threatening skies Holmes and I journeyed to Windsor on Friday afternoon.

Just beyond the Thames Street egress to Windsor's central railway station appears one of the most inspiring scenes in all of England—the grey stone walls and vast green lawns of Windsor Castle. Upon our arrival on this day, however, the gloom in the heavens rendered the panorama darker than usual; and in spite of the imposing view, the entire tableau created in me a sense of foreboding.

Not so with Sherlock Holmes. Despite the urgency of our mission, he was entertaining fond memories. "Do you know, Watson," said he as we gazed up at the castle, "I don't believe I've been to Windsor in over ten years. Not since I had reason to visit the gracious lady who used to hold court here. She bestowed an emerald tie-pin upon me."

I was all for moving forward. Still, I too remembered the reason for Holmes' audience with the Queen, his recovery of the so-called Bruce-Partington Plans. In the wrong hands, the stolen documents containing the design of a secret submarine could have caused disaster for the Royal Navy. The case involved not only espionage at Woolwich Arsenal, but also the murder of a clerk named Arthur Cadogan West who worked there.

"You well deserved the recognition," I said. "Saving those naval plans was a great defence of the country."

"Thank you, Watson, though I must confess that the current situation prevents one from feeling too complacent. In the earlier matter, the Queen herself was not imperilled; on this occasion, the threat to the monarchy is direct."

I had to agree. The King's Garden Party was to take place the next day. With the expected appearance of the Oxford-degree recipients—among them Sam Clemens; his friend and fellow writer, Rudyard Kipling; composer Camille Saint-Saëns; sculptor Auguste Rodin, and the founder of the Salvation Army, General

William Booth—as well as celebrities ranging from the Prime Minister, Sir Henry Campbell-Bannerman, to the famed actress Ellen Terry—the number of attendees within—not to mention the number of gawpers without—would be very large indeed.

"We've done well to arrive before the onslaught," said Holmes. "Beginning at 2:45 tomorrow afternoon, the railway is adding ten special London trains to Windsor."

Earlier in the day, I had explained to Mrs. Watson that business of national importance was taking me to Oxford for much of the weekend. I had then joined Holmes in a taxi, which motored us to Paddington for the railway trip to Windsor. Chief Inspector Hopkins had secured Spartan rooms for us in a small hotel near Peascod Street. If the trouble we encountered in finding a suitable dining establishment that evening was any indication, we were fortunate to have lodgings at all in a city whose population had ballooned in the last day or two. As it was, we ended up with fish and chips in the Book and Candle, a smoke-filled pub that was crowded enough to make bending an elbow a challenge.

"We owe much thanks to Hopkins for getting us rooms," said I over a lager.

Holmes raised his tankard through the haze. "Just as friend Hopkins," said he *sotto voce*, "owes much thanks to *us*, Watson. If our information regarding this threat to the Crown is correct, the constabulary is wise to have us readily available for consultation—if not direct action. The local police will be watching the castle; we shall join them tomorrow."

With soldiers and police in abundance, I couldn't imagine what additional protection Holmes and I might contribute to the welfare of His Majesty. And yet anyone with even the most fleeting knowledge of history can cite numerous examples of royal pride preceding a royal fall.

Chapter Twelve

All that report about my proposal to buy Windsor Castle and its grounds
is a false rumor—I started it myself.
--Mark Twain to King Edward VII
Quoted in *The New York Times*,
June 23, 1907

Rain threatened early Saturday in both London and
Windsor. But no threat of inclement weather in either city could
prevent Sam Clemens and Ralph Ashcroft from pushing their way
through the hundreds of supporters that surrounded Brown's
Hotel that afternoon to secure a cab. Clemens and his secretary
were on their way to Paddington and a 2:45 train departure.

In Windsor, huge crowds were filling Thames Street and
Castle Hill as well. In spite of ever-darkening clouds, the number
of people hoping to catch a glimpse of the famous American
continued to grow. Large throngs forced the queue of motorcars
and four-wheelers to make the brief drive from the station to the
East Lawn of the Castle at a snail's pace. For Clemens, of course,
the longer it took, the more time he could spend enjoying the
open-carriage ride. Accompanied by MP John Henniker Heaton
and his wife, a smiling Clemens would be waving his top hat and
bowing his head at the cheering crowd.

Now the grounds had yet to open, but Holmes and I would
have a clear view of all the goings-on when they did. We, along
with a phalanx of uniformed police and soldiers, were stationed in

a cavernous hall of the Castle overlooking the lawn. The martial nature of the force proved how successfully Stanley Hopkins had conveyed to his superiors the seriousness of the threat posed by Thomas Luck. Hopkins may have been dressed in tweed, but the Chief Inspector stood erect with all the bearing of the uniformed officers surrounding him. Whatever Holmes' reservations, my friend had clearly contacted the right man at Scotland Yard.

"The King wants no overt display of military strength," explained Hopkins as we peered through a massive lead-glass window. "His Majesty fears that such a show would destroy the festive atmosphere that the Royal Family hope to create."

The Chief Inspector scanned the milling crowd. "Look at all the people waiting to get in. Policing such an event on a day when there *is* no specific threat is nightmare enough. That's probably why there hasn't been a garden party at the castle in ten years."

* * *

The gates swung open at three o'clock; and beneath the red, gold, and blue of the Royal Standard flying from the Castle tower, the invitees began to fill the grounds. Men in required cutaways and silk hats and women in white dresses and elaborate *chapeaux* passed through the King's private flower garden on their way to the East Lawn, a dramatic swatch of green bisected by the lengthy pathway called the Long Walk.

Beneath an array of white tents, guests jostled one another for hot tea, finger sandwiches, peaches, strawberries and grapes. Adding to the festivities were tables bedecked with Sèvres china, gold tea services, and exotic flowers from nearby Frogmore Gardens sprouting from gold vases. It was within these same marquees that many of the guests—the richly dressed women, in particular—sought shelter when a light rain began to fall.

An hour passed, and then quite dramatically musical bands from the Grenadier and Horse Guards struck up the National Anthem. Immediately, a certain tenseness quieted all of us in the hall, for everyone within understood the importance of the music—the slow, melodic strains announcing the entrance of the King. As onlookers stretched and twisted to get a glimpse of His Majesty and the Royal Family, the soldiers and police behind the windows scanned the crowds with greater intensity.

King Edward, in top hat and frock coat, a red rose in his lapel, appeared with Queen Alexandra by his side. Her Majesty was elegantly draped in a white fur stole, with splashes of colour most pronounced in the red roses in her hair. The accompanying Royal Family displayed little in the way of martial garb, but the King and Queen were flanked by a number of military men in sharply-pressed dress uniforms. Various officials cleared the way, and the Royals proceeded slowly down the East Lawn. Following designated lanes lined ten deep with devoted throngs (and not a few umbrellas), they made their way to a pair of large, flower-enveloped marquees—one blue, one red—that occupied the centre of the open area near the grand stairs leading from the castle.

I recognized the red canopy as the *shamiana* His Majesty had brought from India. At its base were red roses, white hydrangea and thick smilax bushes of white and green; at the front on poles of beaten-silver hung the flags of Germany, Greece, and Siam in recognition of the Royal Family's guests that day. Next to these standards hung the royal ensign of Great Britain signifying that underneath this particular canopy stood the King and Queen of England.

Chief Inspector Hopkins stared in the direction of the packed pavilions, and Sherlock Holmes examined the crowd with the field glasses the policeman had provided.

"Those smartly-dressed soldiers," said Holmes without looking away from the lenses. "One need only watch their eyes darting about to know they're more than just window-dressing."

Stanley Hopkins nodded. "What's more," said the Chief Inspector, "if the King should be in danger, the men behind us can instantly deploy."

I hoped no one viewed my smirk. Even I, who in spite of some army training am no military tactician, recognized that the King was far enough away so that, if his immediate bodyguards failed to protect him, this well-armed force, regardless of its size, could do even less. At least, one could take comfort that His Majesty was mingling with people who'd actually been invited inside the castle walls. Or so we hoped. The guest list totalled over eight thousand. With such large numbers, one might also fancy how a single invitation—for that was all it would take— could be bought or stolen by some malcontent with evil intentions.

It was no wonder then that Holmes maintained a grim expression whilst handing me the field glasses. For all his searching, he had as yet identified no one resembling Thomas Luck.

"It's your turn," said he, rubbing his eyes. "I need to rest."

There were all manner of faces to ponder. It had been years since we'd last seen Thomas Luck, and who could tell what the fiend looked like today or, for that matter, what kind of disguise he might have conjured? We knew he'd changed his name—why not his appearance as well? He could be that bewhiskered man in the top hat and cutaway. Or that straight-backed officer in a foreign uniform I failed to recognize. Or perhaps the dark-skinned, turbaned gentleman approaching the royal family just now.

Our task was to look for any suspicious or threatening activity. Yet I must confess that on more than one occasion I found myself focusing the field glasses on Sam Clemens in frock coat and top hat as he made his way through the crowd. He'd aged some since last we'd seen him. The hair peeking out from under the hat brim was whiter, the face more lined; and he walked with the slight limp that was most probably due to the gout which had sent him to Nevill's Turkish Baths all those years ago. And yet with bursts of renewed energy he shook hands with as many admirers as he could reach. "CB", the Prime Minister, had been among the first to greet him. Whatever one thought of Clemens personally, one couldn't deny his magnetism.

Later, amidst the flowers that fronted the Royal marquee, American Ambassador Whitelaw Reid officially presented Samuel Clemens of Hannibal, Missouri, to Edward VII, King of England. According to the newspaper reports, Reid had told Clemens at the appointed moment that the writer was "wanted."

"By the police?" Clemens had asked.

"No," the Ambassador answered. "By the King and Queen."

From what I could observe through the field glasses, though he respectfully removed his top hat in addressing the King, Clemens did most of the talking; and His Majesty, in spite of the reported death-threat in the air, did a great deal of laughing.

To his credit, the American commoner seemed very much at ease when conversing with royalty. Clemens had met Edward some fifteen years before at Bad Nauheim in Germany when His

Majesty was still the Prince of Wales, and one can only assume that they had much to discuss about the happenings to both of them during the intervening years. Nonetheless, eyebrows rose when with a suede glove Clemens patted the King on the arm.

It was even more surprising to watch Clemens minutes later, his hat firmly in place on his head, address a seated Queen Alexandra. Afterwards, he would report that Her Majesty had instructed him to keep his head covered to protect his health in case the rain should return. Sam Clemens spent at least a quarter of an hour conversing with His Majesty and the Queen—much longer than did any of the other guests, if I was to be the judge.

Suddenly, I realized I was neglecting my job. An assassin might be on the loose! It took a suspicious-looking chap dressed in pin stripes to remind me of my responsibility. He stood too tall for Luck, but might have been an accomplice. With his top hat pulled down over his brow and black scarf wrapped round the lower part of his face, training the field glasses on him did little to reveal his identity. Even more curious was his right arm, which was nestled in a black sling. So completely enveloped was this limb that the fingers of his hand remained concealed.

"Holmes," said I, still looking through the magnifying lenses, "there's a strange fellow not twenty feet from the King."

I received no answer and turned to look at my friend. Sherlock Holmes was gone.

When I refocused my gaze on the man, he was now mulling about the Royal marquee, apparently sizing up the soldiers and guests. Could this mysterious stranger have been looking for an opportunity to take his place in the queue that led to the Royal family?

It was the thought of the queue that caused me alarm. For the procession reminded me of the line of people a few years

158

before in Buffalo, New York, who were waiting to meet the American President William McKinley. In a manner strikingly similar to the person I was now watching, the anarchist called Leon Czolgosz had appeared in the file with a bandaged right hand. When he came to the head of the line and the President reached out for a fraternal shake, Czolgosz did the same. But instead of clasping McKinley's hand, Czolgosz fired the .32 calibre Iver Johnson revolver he'd been concealing within the folds of the bandage, ultimately killing the President.

Perhaps in style—if not in philosophy—this similarly-bandaged man might be what the Americans call a "copycat".

Panic seized me when I momentarily lost sight of the suspicious figure, and I frantically scanned the crowd to locate him. But then the bands struck up the anthem again. I'd lost track of the time. Somehow, it was already 6:00, and the music signalled that the event was concluding. The King and the Royal family were taking their leave, and fortunately the stranger was nowhere to be seen. I may have sighed audibly, but I kept my glasses focused on the crowds.

Just then, a whisper sounded at my ear: "The instant you think you are safe," it said, "is the instant you become most vulnerable."

I lowered the glasses and stared to my left. Standing next to me was the very person I'd been watching just moments before through my magnifying lenses, the man with the bandaged hand whose hat and scarf had served so admirably in concealing his identity. Rather, I should say that it was Sherlock Holmes who was standing to my left because it was he, I now realized, whom I'd been tracking through the field glasses. I suppose I should have been mightily humiliated; but in truth, I had been fooled by Holmes' disguises on so many occasions that my inability to penetrate one more failed to embarrass me in the least.

All of us in that military encampment breathed more easily when we learned that King Edward, Queen Alexandra, and the rest of the Royal entourage had made their way back to the castle unmolested. With the King safely returned, I took the liberty of asking Holmes, "Why the dressing on your hand? You put me in mind of the assassin, Leon Czolgosz."

"Point well taken, Watson. Actually, it was Czolgosz who gave me the idea. When one prowls through a crowd on the hunt for a possible killer, a large cloth binding provides excellent cover for one's weapon—as Czolgosz sadly demonstrated. Had I needed, I could have fired the pistol in my hand without wasting time removing it from my pocket."

Fortunately, no such reaction had been required. Indeed, a general calm had prevailed throughout the afternoon, which one could attribute to the presence of Samuel Clemens; for in truth, most all the people had kept their eyes on the popular author. It is difficult to fancy anyone upstaging the King of England, and yet—if the attention of the crowd can be taken as a guide—Sam Clemens, for all his American commonality, had accomplished just that.

In retrospect, we were fortunate that Chief Inspector Hopkins was a reasonable man. Having chosen to err on the side of caution, he didn't complain to Holmes about the increase in security and manpower Hopkins had called into play.

"I'm much obliged for your help," he told Holmes at the day's conclusion, yet the furrows in the policeman's brow suggested to both Holmes and me that his appreciation appeared more formal than sincere. One could easily imagine his defence for the dressing down he was likely to receive: "I was misled by Sherlock Holmes' misguided fear of some criminal attack against the King". That any such attack might have been thwarted by the muted but ominous show of force arrayed by the authorities would probably be discounted. In the eyes of Stanley Hopkins, it would have doubtlessly required a Royal tragedy to prove Holmes' supposition correct.

"In spite of my high hopes," observed Holmes later, 'whether Chief Inspector or simple detective, Stanley Hopkins has always seemed to disappoint me."

* * *

The sun was just setting as our train clattered along the rails towards London. Grey clouds tinged with pink washed across the heavens. Holmes' dour expression seemed an appropriate herald for the darkness to come. We should have been feeling great joy in the knowledge the King was safe, but I knew that closing the door on one target opened the door to another. Holmes said much the same. Yet on this occasion, I must confess to bein greatly surprised by the way he said it.

"In American baseball, Watson, a batter is called 'out' on a third missed swing, a third strike. Is that not so?"

I have written elsewhere that my friend's knowledge of contemporary sport was severely limited. This ignorance, however, never seemed to impede his employment of sport metaphors. Resorting to American idiom in reflecting on British royalty might have given someone else pause. But I thought I understood the progression at what Sherlock Holmes was hinting, and I merely raised my eyebrows to encourage him to complete his thought.

"With our worries about the Gold King, Watson, we seem to have swung and missed. We likewise misread the situation regarding His Majesty; that makes two strikes. You know me well enough, old fellow, to appreciate that I have no intention of swinging and missing a third time."

"Right. You want to be like 'Nap' Lajoie'," said I, invoking one of the top baseball players in America.

"Sorry?" Clearly, Holmes had never heard the name. Nonplussed, he sat opposite me swaying with the rhythm of the train.

"Na-*po*-le-on *La*-jo-way," I articulated. A bit of an athlete myself in my younger years—rugby was my passion—I was always eager to display my knowledge of any sport. In point of fact, ever since our recent encounter with the late Stephen Crane, an American writer who'd played baseball in college, I'd taken an interest in learning more about the game. Sometimes I even got my hands on a copy of *The Sporting News*, a small American periodical limited entirely to reports on baseball.

"Lajoie's one of the best," I explained, pleased to pontificate. "He's with Cleveland now; he used to play for Philadelphia."

"I see," said Holmes, flashing a quick and condescending smile. Then he returned to business. "Let us rethink this talk of kings."

But I wasn't finished. "It's funny, Holmes," I persisted. "When I think of baseball, I don't envision strike-outs. I picture players like Lajoie or the 'Georgia Peach'—"

Holmes arched a questioning eyebrow at this last reference.

"Ty Cobb," said I, warming even more to my subject. "He plays for the Detroit Tigers. When I think of such players, I always picture them connecting—not missing. I see the ball flying over a fence somewhere. To become as good as those players are—I mean, really good—they must have practiced for years. I imagine they started hitting balls a long way when they were youths—'homeruns' they're called."

Suddenly, Holmes fixed me with a piercing stare. "What did you say, Watson?"

"'Homeruns', I repeated, thinking that the clatter of the rails must have blocked the word.

"No, no. Before that. What did you call the lads who play baseball at an early age?" His voice was vibrating with energy.

"'Youths'," I repeated.

"A word which might remind you of the nickname Mrs. Clemens gave her husband," said Holmes, grey eyes flashing. "Do you remember?"

I thought for an instant. "Why, 'Youth', I offered.

"That's right, Watson. But there was another nickname for Samuel Clemens as well. Clara Clemens told us that 'Youth' was what her *mother* had called him. There was also a nickname employed by his friend Miss Lyon. Clara frowned at the name and said her mother would never use it. But she also said that Senator Gibson liked it because it tied the two men together. Thomas Luck had worked for the Senator quite a while and must have observed him with Clemens on many occasions. Luck would certainly have known that Miss Lyon called the man—"

Holmes left the completion of the sentence to me.

"—'The *King*'," I volunteered.

"Homerun!" cried Holmes.

Chapter Thirteen

We get our morals from books. I didn't get mine from books, but
I know that morals do come from books—
theoretically, at least.
--Mark Twain
"Remarks at the Opening
of the Mark Twain Library"

"Surely, there must be a printed schedule of Clemens' proposed activities here in England."

Holmes and I were drinking sherry in my sitting room later that night, and he spoke whilst reaching for a copy of *The Times*. Unfolding the paper, he flattened the pages out on the butler's table and began scrutinizing the text.

Suddenly, he looked up and gazed at me with a wounded expression. "You do realize, don't you, Watson, that this research requires me to relive one of my most humiliating defeats. You rightly called the case 'The Problem of Thor Bridge', for a 'problem' it most certainly presented. And still does."

It required no great insight to recognize the ill memories that a new look at the case would dredge up.

"Recall, that it was Clemens—not *I*, the so-called *'professional'* detective—who pointed the finger of guilt at Thomas Luck. No, I was the 'mere mortal' who wrongly concluded that Mrs. Gibson's death had been a suicide. It was Clemens—the *amateur*, if you will—who suspected the truth and, by securing those finger-marks on the glass, exposed Luck as the true killer."

"But after all this time, Holmes—"

He cut me off before I could wish aloud that maybe Clemens had forgot everything about the case, especially his rivalry with Holmes.

"Luck spent years nurturing the vengeance caused by his mother's murder in Hope Canyon; and when he finally put his plan into action, he achieved the near-perfect crime on Thor Bridge. Even more galling, he staged Maria Gibson's suicide as a blind to ensnare overly-clever investigators like me. Had I been more alert, the police could have apprehended Thomas Luck just weeks after he'd killed Gibson's wife. Instead, seven years later, we have him seeking new victims. Give Luck credit, old fellow; he fooled Sherlock Holmes."

"But not Sam Clemens," I felt compelled to repeat.

"Exactly. And to his credit, Clemens appreciated the enormity of his own accomplishment. I understand that now. That's why he so intensely resented the omission of his role in your account of Mrs. Gibson's murder—and why he wrote that infernal story."

"But Conan Doyle—"

"Please, Watson, let's not relive *that* sorry episode. Besides, we don't have the luxury of time."

Holmes looked down at the newspaper once more, and I watched his grey eyes dance across the page. Suddenly, his finger pounced on a spot near the bottom of the right-hand sheet. "Here it is, Watson!"

He muttered as he read, though clearly audible were phrases like "arrival time", "garden party", "talk of extending his stay".

Once he'd digested the list, he announced, "Tuesday—

tomorrow. Clemens speaks tomorrow at the Savoy Luncheon for the Society of Pilgrims."

"'Society of Pilgrims'?"

"An Anglo-American group seeking to strengthen the ties between our countries. It's a relatively small affair—a couple of hundred people at most, I should imagine. Obviously, the primary event, the highlight of Clemens' trip, occurs the next day when he receives his Doctor of Letters degree at the Sheldonian Theatre in Oxford. There will be thousands there."

"Of course," I agreed, "Wednesday morning." That titbit was common knowledge.

"Don't you see? That is where our man will strike. At the Sheldonian."

I shook my head. "How can you be so certain? How do you know that this Thomas Luck won't just try to shoot Clemens down on a street here in London or in a hotel room at Brown's or during that Pilgrims' luncheon at the Savoy you just mentioned?"

Sherlock Holmes reviewed the list once more. "No!" he cried, slapping his hand down on the page. "I'm sure of it. Luck waited all these years for his target to return to England. And no sooner did Clemens arrive than Luck—albeit in a cryptic message about 'the King'—actually forewarned Gibson of his nefarious scheme."

"First Gibson's wife," I observed, "now Gibson's best friend."

"Exactly. Thomas Luck is seeking the right moment; and if my past experiences with deviant minds offer any indication, I am convinced that Luck estimates 'the right moment' to be precisely the time Sam Clemens reaches the pinnacle of his literary career: when the man receives his honorary degree from Oxford University. What could be a more fitting time to kill the man?"

"Surely, we'll notify Scotland Yard."

Holmes snorted. "Watson, do you really think that friend Hopkins wants to hear about the assassination of another 'king'? I know that at some point I told you Hopkins showed promise. But even *I* don't credit the Chief Inspector with having that open a mind."

I was about to say that Hopkins could not go blithely about dismissing the fate of someone with the reputation of Samuel L. Clemens, but Holmes cut me off.

"No, Watson, this is *our* case. It appears that the gods would have me save the life of my most bitter critic. It is just the sort of irony that a satirist like Clemens would relish."

"But what if you're wrong about the location?"

"I'm not. When a killer makes public his intention—however arcane his allusions—one may count on the fact that he regards his upcoming crime as a dramatic performance; and no such performance can be considered successful without an audience."

"A performance? An audience?" I questioned. "The Savoy offers the same opportunities."

"True, but the Sheldonian offers a better one. More people; bigger stage; grander show."

I had to agree. Holmes' reasoning seemed as sound as Luck's seemed mad. Nonetheless, one couldn't afford to ignore Clemens' public appearance at a fashionable hotel.

Holmes agreed. "You do make good points about the Savoy, Watson. There's even the off chance you might be correct. One can't ignore the possibility that some ill-fated act could occur there. That's why I'm asking *you* to follow Clemens to his luncheon. You know what Thomas Luck looks like. There will be some police attending so august a gathering; and if need be—

though I seriously doubt it—you can call upon them to apprehend the villain should he actually materialize.

"I'll go ahead to Oxford and alert the local authorities to our concerns. Assuming no misadventure happens here in London, I'll meet you Tuesday evening at the Sheldonian. The two of us will lie in wait at the theatre the night before the encænia and see if Thomas Luck happens to make an early appearance. Maybe he'll attempt to set up a hide or a lair for his attack. If he does not appear Tuesday night, we'll certainly have to be on our guard the next day during the ceremony itself when his target will be centre-stage."

* * *

Everyone wanted an invitation to the Pilgrims' luncheon at the Savoy—or so it seemed. According to reports, more than a thousand requests had been denied. Fortunately, I happened to know the right person to secure one for me. Whether or not he was a Pilgrim himself, Sir Arthur Conan Doyle maintained relationships with all the right people—including Sam Clemens. Fortunately for Sir Arthur, Clemens seemed not to associate the poor decisions regarding "The Problem of Thor Bridge" with him. What's more, not only had my garrulous agent sent congratulatory seventieth-birthday-wishes to Clemens two years before, but Sir Arthur had also attended the dinner in Clemens' honour at Dorchester House, then the American Embassy, just the previous week.

Yet Sir Arthur was preoccupied with matters other than the adventures of Samuel Clemens. Conan Doyle's wife Louisa had died a year before, and he was now making plans to marry Jean Leakie, a friend for a decade. What's more, Sir Arthur had just played the role of detective himself by recently clearing the name of George Edalji, a young solicitor in South Staffordshire, accused of maiming livestock.

Such concerns consumed much of his time; but Conan Doyle still maintained memberships in any number of prominent societal organizations, which Holmes and I were sure had ties to the Pilgrims. There were his traditional clubs like the Athenæum, as well as newer institutions like the Boz, a group of Dickens enthusiasts; the Authors, a collection of fellow writers; and the Crimes Club, a society of professionals and amateurs fascinated by factual mysteries. In a word, Sir Arthur had plenty of what the Americans like to call "pull".

What's more, he was willing to use it. Once he heard that my request involved a criminal case, he readily agreed to secure my entrance to the Pilgrims' luncheon. With the success of the Edalji matter to spur him on, he was eager to lend a hand in our current investigation. But Sir Arthur was also garrulous; and though appreciative of his help, Holmes and I recognized the need for silence. I would speak to Sir Arthur, but give away as little as possible. He would learn nothing from me of the reason for my surveillance of the Pilgrims or, for that matter, of the necessity for the Webley that I would be concealing inside my jacket. In the end, he promised to get me into the luncheon.

* * *

To this day, the Savoy Hotel commands the only street in London that allows traffic to proceed on the right. Called Savoy Court, the road had been laid out in such a fashion so the various carriages disgorging guests could stop directly in front of the entrance, thereby eliminating the inconvenience to passengers of having to cross a congested roadway in order to enter the establishment.

The motor-car transporting me to the Savoy early Tuesday afternoon joined the string of vehicles in the Strand waiting to turn into Savoy Court. I was too impatient to sit quietly, however; and I told cabman that I would simply exit the motor in the lengthy tail of the queue. I paid the man and alighted, immediately finding myself amongst the jostling and cheering hordes hoping to glimpse Samuel Clemens as he entered the Savoy. With the low roar of the crowd playing in the background, I kept one eye out for Thomas Luck as I made my way towards the hotel entrance.

A doorman liveried in grey top hat and grey frock coat opened the grand doors and ushered me inside. Hoping Conan Doyle had safely secured my admission, I presented my name to a tuxedoed fellow at the entryway to Victoria Hall and, holding my breath as he perused a long list of printed names, quickly exhaled when I was ushered inside a grand chamber.

Pendant chandeliers, wall sconces and table lamps illuminated the twenty round tables that were spread about the hall. The elegantly framed-programs perched on every white-linen tablecloth presented a statement announcing the theme of the Pilgrims' luncheon, the encouragement of England and America to stand "as one in honouring Twain". In addition to announcing a meal of grilled meats and poached salmon, the menu cards presented a drawing of the famed writer in colours of brown, blue, and yellow. Not only did the illustration depict Mark Twain in the broad-brimmed hat and long robes of a religious-style pilgrim, but it also presented him carrying a tall quill pen—presumably not warmed up in hell—in one hand, and in tribute to his most famous short story, a leash attached to a jumping frog in the other.

With the responsibility of protecting Sam Clemens, I did my best to remain in the background. As a result, I could only watch as some two hundred Pilgrims and their guests dined on the previously mentioned delicacies. Whilst slowly skirting the cavernous hall in search of villains, however, I did get to hear the words of the Right Honourable Augustine Birrell, the Chief Secretary for Ireland, who presided over the luncheon. He evoked laughter at the start by referring to the two great divisions of authors, "the living and the dead," and he soared to great heights by calling Mark Twain "a true consolidator of nations." These remarks were followed by a toast to the American, which was echoed by the entire congregation that got to their feet *en masse* to join in.

Acknowledging the cheers, Sam Clemens rose from his seat. With a large, black cigar jutting from his mouth, he struck a classic pose. Yet as he stood alone under his lion's mane of white hair, all I could think of was what a singular target he presented. Clemens, of course, remained ignorant of any danger and began speaking humorously enough in that familiar high-pitched drawl. He referred to the now familiar anecdote regarding the theft of the famous horseracing trophy, the Ascot Cup, that coincided with his arrival in England. As Clemens loved to report, when newspaper headlines announced "Mark Twain arrives; Ascot Cup Stolen", more wags than just Clemens himself chose to view the two events as related. The laughter that erupted when he recounted the story confirmed how many others drew the same conclusion.

Sam Clemens knew how to work an audience; and growing more serious as he progressed, he employed a sometimes powerful and other times soft voice to talk about

England. It was a country that held great meaning for him, for it was here, he reminded the group, that he'd first received word of his daughter Suzy's death. Ultimately, he turned his focus to the Pilgrims themselves. By confessing his affection for the English people—although presumably still excluding Sherlock Holmes—he embodied the ties between the United States and England, the major tenet of the organization itself. Standing beneath the English flag or the American mattered little to him, he said, because beneath either, "I am not a stranger, I am not an alien, but at home."

These last words evoked more applause, and I breathed a bit easier when I realized he'd safely reached the peroration of his speech. He concluded his words by alluding to the doctoral award he was to receive the next day. It was time, said he, looking at his watch, "to catch a train for Oxford".

Thunderous cheering and handclapping marked the conclusion of his talk; but rather than join in the ovation, I reminded myself to remain vigilant. Concealed by the shade of a large potted plant in an archway at the back of the hall, I continued to eye the attendees for any signs of Thomas Luck in particular or suspicious behaviours in general—hoping all the while, as happened to be the case, that I would find neither.

As the group was breaking up and I made my way to the lobby, I heard the familiar high-pitched drawl addressing me.

"Dr. Watson, I presume," said Sam Clemens with a wink. "I thought that was you I spied earlier lurking about in the shadows." Stiffly, he turned his body this way and that to survey the entire room.

I knew whom he was looking for. "Holmes isn't here."

"He's not a Pilgrim?"

"No," I answered. "Nor am I."

The writer's tufted eyebrows rose. Clearly, he was wondering what I was doing there.

"Conan Doyle got me admitted." I contemplated reporting to him the unsubstantiated fears Holmes and I were harbouring when it suddenly struck me that even after all this time Clemens probably had no idea just how deeply "A Double-Barrelled Detective Story" had wounded my friend back in 1902. Though Holmes would have opposed my mentioning anything at all regarding his reaction, I believed that Clemens ought to know.

"Sherlock Holmes was grievously hurt by your short story about him all those years ago," I announced.

Clemens simply shrugged. "I meant no harm. Your friend needs to develop a tougher hide."

"You have the reputation as a humourist," I countered. "Holmes had the expectation of being amused by your story, not of encountering a vicious attack on himself."

Clemens sighed. "Dr. Watson, I think you misunderstand me if all you expect is folly. I've always maintained that the true source of humour is sorrow. Mr. Holmes should not have been seeking uproarious laughter from the likes of me. There's no humour in heaven, you know." He poked me on the lapel to emphasize his last point.

"I would be the last person to argue with *you* about humour, Mr. Clemens. But I believe you've also maintained that the most successful humourists never let on that they're being funny. Perhaps these current protests and denials you're espousing are simply part of your narrator's guise."

He seemed to give my words some thought. Yet with hundreds of people swirling about us, the lobby of the Savoy seemed neither time nor place to prolong a discussion regarding Sam Clemens' humour or Sherlock Holmes' reaction to it—let alone reporting to Clemens on the re-emergence of Thomas Luck.

"I can only tell you," said I with what I hoped was a note of finality, "that both Holmes and I are looking out for your safety."

"Well, thank you," said he and, turning away, was swept up by his secretary, Ralph Ashcroft, in the group of Pilgrims heading towards the exit.

"We were at Windsor too!" I shouted after him. There was no reason to furnish that particular information save wanting to inform the American that Holmes in particular was involved in his protection.

I don't know whether Sam Clemens actually heard those final words of mine. No doubt he wouldn't have understood their significance if he had; but after joining Mr. Ashcroft, he did turn round and give me a quizzical look. Then he was out the door and on his way to catch the 4:55 train for Oxford.

Chapter Fourteen

For twenty years I have been diligently trying to improve my own
literature, and now, by virtue of the University of Oxford, I mean to
doctor everybody else's.
--Mark Twain
Speech at the Savage Club,
6 July 1907

Sam Clemens arrived in the "city of dreaming spires" just
before 7:00 Tuesday evening. He proceeded to meet with a tailor
for final adjustments to the scarlet robes he'd be wearing at the
next day's ceremony. After his fitting, he was visited by a barber
who'd asked to shave him. Perhaps it was due to the tension in
the air or my warning to him at the Savoy; but according to
London's *Daily Graphic* of 27 June, the barber provided written
assurance that he had no homicidal plans to cut Clemens' throat.

* * *

I arrived on a later train. In point of fact, I've been to
Oxford on a number of occasions—to watch my wife's nephews
graduate, to cheer at sporting events, even to consult the Bodleian
Library—but never, I confess, to look for a killer. As planned, I
met Sherlock Holmes in Broad Street across the road from the
Sheldonian Theatre, the seventeenth-century architectural
masterwork designed by Sir Christopher Wren. It was in this

grand hall that Clemens, along with the other honourees, would receive his degree.

The late-evening sun bathed the ubiquitous honey-coloured stone of the Sheldonian in a dusky wash of light. With a floor plan said to have been inspired by an open-air Roman theatre, the anterior section containing the entrance appears a conventional rectangle whilst the semi-circular posterior faces the Broad. A cupola adorns the roof like a sentinel on the battlements.

Sherlock Holmes was waiting for me in deerstalker and inverness cape. He was also carrying his loaded hunting crop, which he sometimes brought along when he expected danger. At the moment, he seemed to be returning the gaze of a number of immense stone busts across the road. Set on concrete plinths, these large heads interrupt the lengthy black-rail fence that parallels the curve of the theatre and extends round and beyond the entire rear section of the building. A variety of flowing beards embellish the various elongated faces; and thanks to the pupils pierced into their wide-set eyes of stone, the sombre miens appear to scrutinize anyone on the Broad who dares approach them.

It has never been established after whom the busts were modelled. Some observers regard the statuary as philosophers; others, as emperors; still others, as apostles. I myself have always liked the title of "metaphysical sages". Whatever their proper designation, on that night in particular the gimlet-eyed worthies viewed a larger-than-usual array of visitors. Most had been attracted to Oxford by the next day's ceremony; but one in particular might actually have slunk by those frozen faces with darker, more nefarious plans in mind.

"Ah, Watson," Holmes greeted me. "Welcome to Oxford."

Behind him stood a small pub called The White Horse. Earlier in the day, my duties at the Savoy had forced me to ignore the victuals that were served, and I suddenly realized I was hungry.

"Do you intend to eat before we begin our vigil?" I asked.

"The thought hadn't crossed my mind."

"A moment," said I, holding up my index finger and then stepping quickly into the pub. A few minutes later, I returned with a pair of ham sandwiches wrapped in newsprint.

"Sustenance from The White Horse," I announced and handed Holmes a sandwich.

"We'll eat while walking," said he, accepting the food as an afterthought. "I hope to maintain an uninterrupted view of the theatre tonight."

I nodded, unwrapping my feast.

"You're armed, I assume."

"Yes," I answered, patting my hip pocket, "but surely we're not here alone. What about the police?"

He took a bite of the sandwich and nodded. "I've already explained our concerns to Chief Inspector Wheat of the Oxfordshire Constabulary. He's agreed to keep special watch throughout the night not only on the theatre but also on the route of tomorrow's procession that begins at Magdalen College. The Chief Inspector's also agreed to have two of his men follow Clemens about for as long as he's in Oxford."

"What about the theatre itself?"

"Wheat told me that the police searched the interior this afternoon. He reassured me that they checked every seat, every platform, every crevice. But he also told me that we can look again if we so desire."

"Wouldn't we simply be redundant?"

Holmes shook his head. "The theatre holds four thousand and has lots of nooks and crannies. I thought that a second examination on our part was called for—especially once I told Wheat about Windsor. As I anticipated, after I'd explained our previous attempt to protect a 'king', Wheat spoke to friend Hopkins."

"And Hopkins told him all about the fiasco at the Castle."

"Indeed. As a result, Wheat seems not to be taking my report of the threat against Clemens as seriously as one might wish. Oh, he's cooperating and undertaking thorough searches; but I suspect that he'd be just as happy to allow the bulk of the responsibility to fall upon me."

Holmes pointed to the open gate.

"Let's walk round the theatre so you can get the lie of the land. Then we shall signal a constable to let us inside. At least, that much has been pre-arranged."

Sandwiches in hand, Holmes and I crossed the road, passed through the gate, and mounted the few steps to the grey pavement that surrounds the Sheldonian. From here, unobstructed by the fencing or other buildings, we could circumnavigate the entire theatre.

Eating as we walked, we slowly made our way along the west side, between the Sheldonian and the Old Ashmolean, a multi-windowed, seventeenth-century edifice that has served as a museum over the years.

"What exactly are we looking for, Holmes?"

"It's hard to say. After I forced myself to read that drivel again, the piece by Clemens—"

"'The Double-Barrelled Detective Story'?"

"The same—I wanted to confirm my memory that dynamite plays a significant role in the plot, which it does. And

178

that bit of evidence got me to think that perhaps Luck might be planning to blow up the Sheldonian with Clemens inside it."

"Blow up the Sheldonian?" I scoffed. "You can't be serious. The building's a gem! One of Wren's first commissions." Yet I immediately found myself glancing wildly at the surrounding structures, so many built with seventeenth-century niches and recesses in which a villain might secret away explosives, let alone himself.

My friend laughed softly. "Do you really think that considerations about Christopher Wren permeate the brain of a murderer, Watson? Still, you may rest assured. Before your arrival, I searched high and low outside the theatre for long fuses that might have been laid in advance. Or for signs of excavations where one might plant a device. Or even for nearby rooms from where sticks of dynamite could be thrown."

"And you've found nothing," said I as we passed the Divinity School, "or else we wouldn't still be on duty like this."

"Yes, Watson, that's correct. Nor have I found any evidence of a sniper's perch—at least, not one set up in advance. It leads me to the conclusion that—just as I had expected—whatever's going to happen will happen tomorrow during the event itself. It is for then that we must be prepared."

Nodding, I swallowed the last of my sandwich. "And where is Clemens tonight?" I managed to ask.

To our right loomed various university offices. On the street corner nearest to us paced one of the uniformed constables whom Wheat had assigned to police the area. In the distance the angular Bridge of Sighs arched gracefully over New College Lane.

"That's information I *do* have," said Holmes, finishing his meal as well. "This evening, Clemens is speaking at Jesus College, and he's spending his nights in Oxford at the home of Sir Robert Porter of *The Times.*

"Sir Robert Porter?"

"Sir Robert's lived in the States and at one time served as some sort of commissioner for President McKinley."

"Even so—is Clemens safe in a private home?"

"The police are watching the house, so we should expect no problems there. But here at the Sheldonian? With a stage like this one surrounded by thousands of people, who can say what a madman might attempt?"

By then our perambulations had brought us back to the large busts. "And for that reason," said Holmes, "we shall spend the night out here on the Broad."

However much I may have missed a soft bed, I wasn't surprised.

"Before we begin another round," said Holmes, signalling the constable at the street corner, "let's go inside."

With no great haste, the policeman crossed the road and trudged up the stairs to the front entrance of the theatre. Upon unlocking the door, he nodded at Holmes and let us in. Thanks to the rows of varied windows—some curved, some circular, some round—enough sunlight spilled in to illuminate a wood interior of browns and greys supported by pillars coloured to look like dark marble.

On the ceiling high above, a burst of bright colour caught my attention.

"An allegory by Robert Streeter," Holmes announced, "from the time of Charles II."

Staring upward, I beheld a red celestial sky surrounded by what looked to be all manner of classical-looking figures—some winged, some caped—in the act of expelling even darker creatures from the heavenly scene.

"Note how those gilded strips of wood break up the ceiling into squares and triangles. The wood is supposed to resemble cords with the intent of rendering the entire ceiling an outdoor awning."

"Holmes," I cried, "it is not like you to take an interest in art."

"On the contrary, Watson. I am very much interested in any endeavour that seeks to dramatize, as this work does, the triumph of knowledge over ignorance."

"Our very target tonight," I observed as Holmes and I made our way to the centre of the hall.

At the front, numerous wooden chairs and a speaker's platform had been positioned in preparation for the next day's event. Holmes and I took separate aisles, and up and down the rows we marched, looking on, round, and under the various seating accommodations. There appeared no shortage of places to hide all sorts of infernal devices.

Holmes pointed to the highest galleries, those commonly called "the gods", and we mounted the stairs and perused the upper tiers. We examined the organ in the south gallery with its towering black pipes and gilded carved cherubs and long, narrow-necked horns. We even climbed the wooden staircase to the eight-sided cupola. Beyond its windows there was much to see of Oxford, but nothing related to our search.

It was now well past 9:00; and confident that we'd been as thorough as possible, we exited the theatre and secured the doors. Darkness was approaching; and once again Holmes and I began walking our circuitous route: round the theatre, past the buildings, back to the statues.

By the time we'd completed our latest journey, the skies had grown dark, and the streets had quieted. The White Horse was soon to close its doors, and a few tipsy patrons from there and elsewhere staggered down Broad Street. A bottle crashed somewhere in the darkness. It took another half-hour for the roads to empty, but at last the carriages disappeared, the motorcars departed, the revellers went home, and the moonless night became silent. Occasionally, we'd hear a rustling or scurrying from this corner or that as some nocturnal creature scuttled about.

To me, all seemed in order. No one could have slipped through the police and then past the two of us and got into the building. Still we trod on. Slowly circling the theatre again, we continued our vigil throughout the night, our progress now marked only by the large stone heads standing silent vigil in the darkness.

* * *

Dawn, Wednesday, 26 June: Under dark clouds two uniformed constables positioned themselves on either side of the Sheldonian Theatre—where I would have had them stationed all night. As explained to us by Chief Inspector Wheat, the ceremony was scheduled to begin at 11:00, but the theatre would be filling up well before the starting time. With the doors set to open at 10:00, the queue had begun forming as soon as the sky showed signs of light. In addition, gawpers filled the streets, milling about the theatre or seeking the best vantage points along the route of the upcoming procession. Many carried cameras; some pedalled by on bicycles. With uniform brown shoes, Norfolk jackets, and rolled trouser-bottoms, students were easy to identify.

"I trust that we can now leave matters here at the Sheldonian in the hands of the police," said Holmes. Striding down the Broad, he added, "It's time we were off to Magdalene."

In spite of a night of watchfulness, Sherlock Holmes looked fit and trim. I tried rubbing wakefulness into my eyes as I trailed slowly after him.

Beneath the tall square bell tower, the grand wood gate at Magdalen College, the starting point for the morning's procession, opens onto the High Street east of Catte. It had just gone 8:00 by the time we arrived, and a few dons in black gowns and scarlet hoods were already assembling in the airy Front Quadrangle inside the gateway. At the same time, crowds were forming on both sides of the High.

As minutes ticked off, the number of gowned academicians grew. Soon, like a flock of multi-coloured birds, the participants in all their variegated plumage gathered together in the Hall at Magdalene where fruit, biscuits and wine were being served on long tables. Not all of them came to eat, however. Holmes touched my arm and with a slight nod indicated a shadowy archway across the quadrangle. Within the gloom, I could discern two scarlet-cloaked figures shrouded in a grey haze. They seemed ghostlike at first; but after an instant I clearly recognized the thick, broad moustaches on each. Like a pair of naughty lads in the far corner of a schoolyard, Sam Clemens and Rudyard Kipling were getting in their final smokes before the start of the official assembly.

The procession was scheduled to begin at 10:30, but it was closer to eleven when in a simple black gown the bedel stepped out before the open gates. Holding before him the ancient silver Mace, he strode to the middle of the High Street, paused for a moment, turned right, and then began his slow and deliberate march down the road that would lead to the Sheldonian. Next came the heads of colleges and then, in double file, the Oxford dons. Arranged by complicated and arcane rankings, they appeared in their flat or soft black caps and flowing gowns of scarlet and either black or salmon or grey. Next came the honourees, thirty or so robed in scarlet, and slowly marching in double file. It was for this august group that all the pomp and circumstance had been created. At the "tail of the herd," as Mark Twain had written of another such congregation, came Clemens and Kipling.

Once Holmes and I had located Sam Clemens, we too were on the move, Holmes appropriating the south side of the road; I, the north. Our goal was to shadow the slow advance of the procession as it maintained its measured pace along the High. Applause and cheers filled the sidewalks, and we had to elbow our way through the push and pull of enthusiastic well-wishers and their seemingly endless supply of furled parasols, bulky picnic baskets, and assorted box-cameras. Looking for Thomas Luck in such a crowd seemed like searching for the proverbial needle in a haystack.

When the procession reached Catte Street, there emerged through the wooden gates of All Souls to lead the group the erect figure of Lord Curzon, the Chancellor of Oxford University. Partially due to a childhood spinal injury, His Lordship, former Viceroy of India and former Foreign Secretary, moved stiffly and slowly in a black gown bedecked with gold braid and various colourful medals. Behind him, strode two young lads in black, who held up the end of Lord Curzon's train. Cheers greeted the dignitaries as the line turned right, passed the circular Radcliffe Camera, and then swung left onto the Broad. So far, all seemed well; the procession had reached the final leg of the march, and still we had not the slightest hint of any trouble.

Huzzahs were constant throughout the route, but I would be less than accurate if I didn't report that the ovations grew louder, the kodaking more frequent, whenever Clemens' shaggy white locks and drooping moustache came into view. The ceremony may have been British in nature, but there was no doubt that the day belonged to the American. No sign of gout now, Sam Clemens of Hannibal, his scarlet skirts billowing behind him like great red wings, preened along the streets of Oxford as proudly as any septuagenarian had walked anywhere before him. Blue eyes twinkling, he would raise his black mortarboard and wave his appreciation to the crowds that were cheering him on. One could chart the man's progress by noting where the cheers turned into roars.

In the midst of all this gaiety, Holmes and I continued our search for a fiend. Nor were we alone. The uniformed police presence was obvious, and detectives in mufti also roamed freely through the crowds. But every one of us knew that you can't stop a madman bent on mayhem if the luck of the draw doesn't place you directly in line with the villain at just the right moment.

Lord Curzon had now reached the first of the sculptured heads in front of the Old Ashmolean. A few statues later, and he would arrive at the entrance gate to the theatre; a few more steps would bring him to the portal leading inside. Suddenly, the sun burst out from behind the clouds; and at the same instant, as if on cue, the mighty strains of "God Save the King" began to swell within the theatre.

The Chancellor waited for the anthem to conclude and then, with a final wave of acknowledgement to the cheering spectators, disappeared inside. The boys carrying his train immediately followed, as did the string of professors in their various coloured robes. It had just gone a quarter past eleven.

So intent was I on spotting Thomas Luck that I was taken aback at the sight of another familiar face. I was approaching the Sheldonian on the north side of the Broad when amongst an array of blossoming parasols, I suddenly recognized the Gold King across the road standing just outside the gate to the theatre grounds. Gibson, in a light-coloured summer suit, was accompanied by his wife Grace, wearing a dress of powder blue. With the two children—now some seven years older than the tots I'd been envisioning—gaily attired in seasonal boating costumes, the entire family appeared ready for summer fun whilst Holmes and I tracked an assassin.

I would learn later that the Gold King had arranged for the family to take their seats in the Sheldonian after they'd cheered Sam Clemens marching past. And indeed the increased roars now told the Senator that for the initial glimpse of his long-time friend he should train his eyes no longer on those dignitaries strutting directly before him but rather down the street where the remaining honourees were still parading.

Sam Clemens had already turned the corner and was now approaching the great stone heads. Then he was past the Old Ashmolean and nearing the gates. At first sight, I didn't perceive the small man on the other side of the street. He'd been shielded by the numerous bodies in the crowd; but just as Clemens was about to step up to the theatre grounds, I espied behind the front line of cheering people the face I had been seeking all morning. It was bewhiskered and lined and partly concealed by a wide-brimmed straw hat and smoked glasses; but despite the passage of time I recognized it immediately. The face belonged to Thomas

Luck, Marlow Bates, the devil incarnate, who was just now reaching inside the lapel of his tweed coat.

Where's Holmes? I can't see Holmes! He'd been walking parallel to Clemens on the same side of the street as Luck, and yet I couldn't locate him.

Elbows out, I pushed my way through the crowd. Even though I knew I could never reach Clemens before he converged with Luck, I lunged forward, and that was when I saw my friend. Holmes too had marked the assassin and was pushing and shoving his way through the throngs to intercept him. The more Holmes pushed, however, the more he was blocked; for the crowd was being driven to near frenzy by the immediate appearance of Sam Clemens. I shouted encouragement; but even had Holmes been able to hear me, I realized full well that he too was not close enough to help.

Suddenly, Luck burst through the wall of cheering spectators and fired his pistol at the smiling old man in the scarlet robes.

* * *

In the Senator's younger years, the man then called Jed Gibson had known guns and action. Now in the blink of an eye at the gates to the Sheldonian, he saw Thomas Luck whip out his pistol just behind him, and he recognized Sam Clemens as its target. We shall never know if Gibson had even a moment to think about it—whether he'd had the time to weigh the life of a wealthy husband and father, a former United States Senator, against that of an aging author beloved by all the world. What we do know is that in that blink of an eye, he stepped between the weapon and the target.

The enraged gunman was already in the act of squeezing the trigger. He fired three times, and three bullets punctured Gibson's chest. At the sharp reports, Clemens himself staggered backward, but was immediately righted by Kipling and moved along by others in the procession towards the gangway leading into the theatre. Amidst shouts and screams, Sherlock Holmes bounded into the scene like a tiger and swung his heavy hunting crop down onto Luck's wrist, knocking the gun to the pavement. An instant later, Holmes had wrestled the small assassin to the ground.

By the time I reached them, Holmes was sitting astride the wretch, pinning him down with the crop laid firmly across Luck's chest. It took the police just moments to arrive. A number of the uniformed constables who'd been patrolling the streets were quick to keep the crowd back; Chief Inspector Wheat himself handcuffed the assassin, and another detective carefully picked up the revolver.

In spite of all this mayhem surrounding the villain, my own thoughts centred on Gibson.

"Make way!" I shouted. "I'm a doctor!"

Darting amongst the frightened people, I scrambled to locate the prostrate victim. When I reached him, I found his head already cradled in Mrs. Gibson's arms. A stream of blood was trailing down from his chest and pooling beneath them. I took his wrist and felt an ever-weakening pulse.

The poor man struggled to look up at us. "Bates," he whispered. "That was Bates who shot me, wasn't it?"

I nodded.

"Why?" he was barely able to whisper.

I didn't have an answer. Even if I had, I suspect he would no longer have been able to hear it. The man who'd started out as a miner of gold and silver clutched his wife's hand and whispered, "Tell Sam. I tried to balance the scales." Those were his final words.

* * *

The awarding of degrees at the Sheldonian continued at the same time Thomas Luck was being shoved into a cell in the Oxford police station. It was to that gaol that Holmes and I went as soon as the authorities took charge on the street.

Chief Inspector Wheat approached us when we arrived. He was now in shirtsleeves; his blond hair stood askew; and lines of worry creased his brow. He seemed to know that Holmes hoped to talk with Bates.

"He wants to speak with *you*, Mr. Holmes. He says that he has a tale to tell. But only to you, you and Dr. Watson."

"With your permission, of course, Chief Inspector," said Holmes.

"Whatever you wish, sir. Had I listened to you from the start and assigned more men, perhaps this tragedy could have been averted."

Holmes offered no response, and the chief inspector turned towards a uniformed officer. "Take these gentlemen to see the prisoner."

Chapter Fifteen

What a curious thing a "detective" story is. And was there ever one that
the author needn't be ashamed of, except
"The Murders in the Rue Morgue"?
--Mark Twain
Notebooks

Through a small, barred window, a shaft of summer
sunlight illuminated the diminutive form of Thomas Luck. His
gaol cell was much brighter than the other lock-up I associated
with the Byzantine story begun on Thor Bridge so many years
before, the gloomy chamber where Grace Dunbar had been
imprisoned in Winchester's foreboding Assizes.

Luck sat at the edge of his cot still wearing the blood-
spotted white shirt and tweed trousers in which he'd been
apprehended, his grizzled beard and thinning hair rendering him
older than his years. He moved very little, but his glance kept
jumping round the cell. A wooden bucket for slops occupied the
far corner.

Just inside the massive oaken door that faced the line of
cells, a uniformed constable stood vigil. Once we'd entered, he
indicated a pair of three-legged, wood stools; and Holmes and I
placed them far enough from the bars at the front of Luck's cell so
that the demented murderer couldn't reach out and grab us if his
demons somehow demanded he try. The policeman, hands
behind his back now and gaze fixed straight ahead, continued to
guard the door.

"As you know," Holmes said to the wild-eyed man in the cell, "we are neither police nor lawyers, so you can speak freely. You came to us once in Baker Street, and much of what you said then—certainly, not all of it—was true. So here's the opportunity to set the rest of the story right."

Luck raised his brows and jerked his head at the policeman. "What about *him*?"

Holmes turned round. "Constable, we'd prefer that you remain outside."

"Right you are, Mr. Holmes," said the guard, snapping to attention. "Chief Inspector Wheat told me to do as you asked. I'll be in the corridor should you require my assistance." He pivoted and exited, shutting the door behind him with a muffled thud.

Holmes and I stared at the imprisoned man. In spite of his darting eyes, he looked less agitated than he had when he'd been arrested. And much less threatening. We sat in silence for a minute or two waiting for Luck to gather his thoughts—or his courage.

Finally, his glance came to rest on my partner. "I do have a story to tell, Mr. Holmes," said he. His accent sounded more English than I'd remembered, but his phrases and vocabulary still echoed his native American speech. "I've been wronged, you see. My past may not justify to you what I've done, but somebody needs to understand."

Holmes stared grimly at the man. "We're listening."

For an instant, Luck's gaze turned heavenward as if for inspiration, and Holmes and I leaned forward to hear all the better. Only on the fewest of occasions did we interrupt his macabre narrative.

* * *

191

"Not even at the start did I intend to kill the son of a bitch. Oh, once I'd learned Gibson's story, I certainly hoped to ruin his life—and I never ruled murder *out* of my thinking—just not *his*. Death would have allowed him to get off too easily.

"It's all about revenge, Mr. Holmes—revenge, if you can believe it, hatched from reading a work of fiction. Had I not taken that literature class back in '83, I would never have embarked on my present path, for I would never have seen that goddam story by Bret Harte—"

"'The Luck of Roaring Camp'," Holmes said. Bret Harte had died five years before, but here was that story again. I'd read it not long after Holmes had done so at the British Museum back in October of 1900.

"Yes, Mr. Holmes," sighed Thomas Luck, slowly shaking his head. "Had I never seen that story, a number of unfortunate souls might have been spared. But, in fact, I *was* assigned to read it, and nothing has been right in my head ever since. For having read it, I couldn't help but realize that Bret Harte's supposed piece of fiction was actually the true history of my own beginnings."

What a bizarre discovery, I thought—*to realize that though you are, in fact, a living being, you are nonetheless regarded by thousands of readers as a make-believe character in literature.*

Luck told us that at first he tried to convince himself that Harte's narrative was not his own. He clung to the inaccuracies in the tale to fool himself—a different name for the mining camp, an earlier timeframe, and especially the baby's death at the end. And yet there were just too many overriding similarities for him to ignore: the mother who died in childbirth, the kind-hearted miners who raised the child, the elusive gold found so soon after the baby's arrival. "Even the fact that I was raised on ass's milk,"

Luck added, "Harte got that right too."

I couldn't help but smile at the detail.

"I have to give him credit," said the prisoner. "Bret Harte understood how the men linked my advent to their discovery of riches. They were a superstitious lot, those men—hence, my surname. As for the melancholy ending—well, all I can say is that Harte seemed to know exactly how to engage his readers. His emotional account of the little fellow's death even moved *me* to tears. I suppose irony can't get any better than that.

"In fact, Bret Harte knew more than he realized. He had the baby drown in the arms of the miner called Kentuck. And in reality, Kentuck's the man I've always considered most like a father to me!"

Luck reported how, when Hope Canyon had played out, he and Kentuck moved to Sacramento and how the boy eventually went on to attend the state university in Berkeley. It was there that an English professor introduced him to "The Luck of Roaring Camp", and once the boy returned to Sacramento, he demanded that Kentuck explain the mysterious coincidences.

Thomas Luck paused again, this time picking at a tuft of straw that had poked through the worn cover of his mattress. He pulled the tuft out of the bedding, examined it, and tossed it to the floor.

"While I was growing up," he began again, "Kentuck and the others discussed among themselves what they figured I needed to know about my birth. It amounted to telling me that my mother had died when I was born and that all the men in Hope Canyon had voted to raise me themselves. Concealing the other facts until I was old enough to ask made a great deal of sense to them. When the time came and I was ready, I turned to Kentuck; and my first question was how the story of my life came to be written by a man named Bret Harte.

"That was when I first learned about Stumpy's visit to the Gillis cabin on Jackass Hill. Kentuck had pieced together all that happened from what Stumpy had told him and from the series of events that followed."

Holmes nodded. "We learned most of this from Bret Harte."

Luck went on as if Holmes hadn't commented. "With Stumpy's saddlebags filled with all sorts of expensive baby things—a silver cup, a silver spoon, a silver-backed mirror—one of the Gillises naturally asked him what a mining camp needed with such stuff. Well, the question set Stumpy off, and he proceeded to tell everyone in the cabin—to boast, really—about the baby he and the others were raising out in Hope Canyon. That's how my story first became public. Obviously, Stump shouldn't have said anything about me at all. Still, he had no reason to worry since he believed he was simply sharing secrets with friends.

"But here's the thing: he didn't pay attention to his audience. Once he realized that two of the strangers in question were writers, he had to ask those fellows—to beg them, really— not to spill the truth to anybody else. Stump breathed more easily when the men agreed." Luck snorted in derision. "At least, Clemens kept his word. We all know how Harte's pledge worked out."

"I don't condone Harte's behaviour," said I. "A true gentleman doesn't break his word. But as an author myself, I can understand his thinking. He told us years ago how confident he was that the story would be a success."

Thomas Luck sprang to his feet. "That hypocritical bastard!" he shouted. "I should have killed him when I had the chance!" Holmes and I instinctively leaned back as Luck ranted at the mere hint of anything good heading Bret Harte's way. "He deserved nothing! He promised Stumpy he wouldn't tell another soul!"

I nodded whilst Holmes simply stared at the madman. So here was the genesis of Luck's grievance against the writer; here was the catalyst for Luck's trip to Lancaster Gate to kill Bret Harte. Fortunately for Sam Clemens, Luck didn't seem to know that "A Double-Barrelled Detective Story" also echoed details from the assault of Luck's mother in Hope Canyon.

"In all fairness," Holmes put in, "Harte himself confessed his transgression."

"So what?" the prisoner huffed, settling himself back on the cot. "Stumpy swore that Harte looked him straight in the eye and said he'd keep his mouth shut. You know what Kentuck said? 'Harte never said nothin' 'bout not usin' his *pen*.' Anyway, I don't need to tell you that, thanks to Bret Harte, the story was soon all over the country.

"But that wasn't the *worst* part." Luck's voice was taking on the rise and fall of melodrama. "You see, Bret Harte and Sam Clemens weren't the *only* strangers visiting the cabin on Jackass Hill the day Stumpy played storyteller. There was *another* fellow listening to the tale—also a friend of the Gillises, or he wouldn't have been there—and he was sitting in the shadows."

"Bret Harte remembered much the same," murmured Holmes.

"As Kentuck told it," continued the prisoner, "this third stranger was sitting on a barrel in a dark corner where you couldn't see him too well, and he was all bewhiskered and dirty. He was certainly nobody Stump recognized. In fact, Stump wouldn't even swear there actually was anybody else in the cabin besides the Gillis brothers, Clemens and Harte. Not that you can blame Stump. He'd never seen that other man wearing a beard. When that fellow wasn't working a mine, he generally appeared as he had on the first day he'd arrived in Hope Canyon: his face clean-shaven; his hair cut short; his store-bought clothes looking fancy."

Luck now took a deep breath. "Could I get some water?"

I rose and walked to the door, all the while pondering the identity of the mysterious stranger in the cabin. Clean-shaven? Refined appearance? And still a miner? I had my theory about who he was, but better to hear it from Luck himself. I knocked for the constable's attention and conveyed the prisoner's request. The policeman returned a few moments later and handed me a dented metal cup half filled with water. I carefully passed it between the bars to Luck. He took a long drink, savoured the liquid, and then returned the cup to me. I put it on the floor next to my stool.

* * *

Thomas Luck swallowed hard. Sitting on both hands, he swayed slowly back and forth. Still rocking, he began again:

"Kentuck apologized before serving up the facts. I'd always thought that my mother was a poor soul named Sally who'd just stumbled into camp one day—the other men had told me as much. Now I learned that she hadn't come alone. The truth, Kentuck warned, was brutal. He called my mother 'a half-breed whore named Cherokee Sal who showed up one day in Hope Canyon with a cruel-eyed dandy'."

Luck's nostrils flared, and his cheeks flushed.

"Kentuck told me that she was a stunner—part Cherokee,

196

with long black hair, dark skin, and a piercing gaze."

I nodded in response; Holmes remained stone-faced.

"I wasn't surprised to hear that she was beautiful. I'd never forgotten the details the men had originally furnished me—how soft her voice was, how pretty her smile—and each new fact added to the portrait in my head. It was like completing a puzzle. I didn't care about her so-called sins; to me, she represented the best there could be in a woman."

Luck shrugged. "I imagine she also looked beautiful to Jed Gibson, for that was the name of the tall, good-looking man with whom she'd arrived in camp."

"My word!" I said in astonishment. "Why, he—"

Holmes cut me off. "Let him continue, Watson."

I held my tongue. Oh, I'd suspected right along that Gibson had been the bewhiskered mystery man who'd been listening to Stumpy's story. The miner hadn't recognized him, but Gibson's presence established the connection between the Senator and Thomas Luck that Holmes and I had been seeking. That much seemed clear. What I hadn't dared to conclude until now was that Gibson was also the well-dressed man who'd arrived in Hope Canyon with the beautiful Cherokee Sal, the same brute who had so viciously attacked the woman and left her for dead in the snow—in short, the man who had killed Thomas Luck's mother.

"Finally, I got to hear the story from its beginnings," Luck said. "At first, the two-faced savage had acted kindly towards her. Gibson met Sal in some brothel in Virginia City months before he set out for the mines. The two of them conducted their so-called business, did some drinking, and eventually moved into a hotel room together. He paid her all the while and talked her into running off to Hope Canyon with him to go look for gold. She'd bring him *luck*, he told her—prophetic words, as it turned out."

"Ironical too," I murmured.

"Kentuck said you could tell by the look in Sal's eyes how much she loved him. But in the end you could also tell—whenever Gibson shoved her away—that what the bastard really wanted was to be free of her. Especially once she'd confessed to him that she was carrying his child."

Kentuck told Luck that Gibson used to drink a lot. Apparently, he'd slap Sal around when he was drunk and sometimes even when he was sober. When he learned she was pregnant, he began using his fists. The other men tried to calm him down, but he'd have no part of their peace making. "I went to law school!" he'd say over and over. "If I don't find any gold, I'll go practice law and settle down and raise a family." And then he'd say to Sal, "You can't do that with some Washoe whore like you who lifts her skirts for any stranger that flashes a gold coin in front of her."

"Kentuck was quick to apologize," Luck said. "'Them's *Gibson's* words,' he'd explained."

The prisoner needed to pause. His eyes were glistening, and he rubbed them with the base of his palms. "In years past," he said, "my eyes would tear up whenever I recalled how badly that man had treated my mother. But whether they were tears of sadness or rage, I couldn't say—not then, anyhow."

At long last, Luck got to the worst part—how during Gibson's final night in Hope Canyon, he'd stripped Luck's pregnant mother naked, tied her to a tree, beat her senseless, and left her to die in the cold—a horrific description that evoked, it must be said, the almost identical scene at the start of Clemens' story belittling Holmes. Clemens' vow of silence regarding what he'd heard on Jackass Hill suddenly seemed less stringent than he'd implied.

"No one ever saw the killer again," Luck murmured. With

a chuckle he added, "Not in Hope Canyon, anyway."

Holmes and I exchanged glances whilst Luck stared down at the floor. We'd seen him commit a brutal murder earlier in the day, and yet the sadness enveloping his life's story evoked a kind of sympathy.

It was a couple of hours later, Luck said, that the men of Hope Canyon found the poor woman half-dead. They removed the ropes, covered her with thick blankets, and carried her into the nearest cabin. They washed away the blood, nursed her back to consciousness, and gave her some food.

Now Luck offered a thin smile. Perhaps it mirrored the features of his mother.

"No son should ever have to conjure so terrible a picture," he declared. "No son should ever have to hear the words I heard from Kentuck. For years, I'd thought my mother had simply died in childbirth! Then all of a sudden I was learning about her humiliation, her horrible death that resulted from that coward's beatings, and to make matters worse, the final indignity—the disappearance of the son of a bitch who'd done all this to her. The more I discovered, the more I could feel the hate inside me grow."

Sherlock Holmes and I sat quietly as Thomas Luck stared at the floor. Then the prisoner raised his head. His eyes looked wildly at the two of us. "They'd been together for almost a year!" he cried. "Do I have to say the words? Jedidiah Gibson, the bastard who murdered my mother? He is—was—my father. My *father*—dare I even pronounce the word?"

"Good God," I whispered as the twisted motivation for the murder on Thor Bridge now flashed through my mind.

How Gibson's insides must have burned in the Gillis cabin as he listened to Stumpy describe the birth of Gibson's son and the death of the baby's mother. It was a tale of horror featuring

Gibson himself as its satanic villain

"I vowed that Jedidiah Gibson would pay," announced Thomas Luck, pressing his hands together. "What's more, I was already formulating my plans. I would hunt down the murderous swine and avenge my mother's murder. She may not have been a saint, but I know she would have cared for me. I know she would have given me the kind of home I'd hoped for." Here he held up his index finger. "Don't get me wrong, gentlemen: the men of Hope Canyon were good to me—very good—but I longed for my mother. What child doesn't? Jedidiah Gibson had taken her from me; and as a consequence, Jedidiah Gibson would have to pay.

"Kentuck feared the gleam in my eye, but I reassured him that I'd finish school and get my sheepskin. What I didn't tell him was that after I'd graduated, I would hunt down my mother's killer."

Suddenly, Thomas Luck slumped, lowering his chin to his chest. Holmes and I must have been the first persons with whom he'd shared his story, and we watched him closely. He sat on his hands once more, a position that somehow seemed to infuse him with strength. A minute later, his back grew straight again, and he raised his head.

"Once I left the university," he said, "I began searching for man. I travelled around the old mining camps in the Sierras, trying to track the son of a bitch. Nobody knew anything, of course. The miners in Hope Canyon did their best to help me by spreading the word that they'd pay in gold for any news regarding Gibson. But no credible reports ever came back.

"It was only much later that I learned what'd become of him following that fateful day on Jackass Hill—the day he'd heard for himself not only what had happened to my mother, but also that he had a surviving son. Pledges to the contrary, he must have realized that the story would get out—it was too dramatic not to. He also had to figure that I was growing up and that sooner or later I too would learn what he'd done to my mother. Gibson had lived out West where people believed in 'Frontier Justice', and the man rightly reasoned that it was high time for him to get out of California.

"In fact, what the coward did was to leave the country completely. With the money he'd made from selling his stake in a California gold mine, he paid for a steamship ticket to Brazil. He must have figured that South America was far enough away for him to be safe."

This part of Luck's story coincided with what I'd heard years before from the Senator himself at Nevill's Turkish Baths.

"Only God can explain why good fortune sometimes shines on villains," Luck philosophized, "but as I suspect you're already aware—the story is common knowledge, after all—the man discovered gold in Brazil, became fabulously rich, and started calling himself 'J. Neil Gibson' instead of 'Jed'. He married a hot-blooded young beauty named Maria Pinto with whom he returned to America. J. Neil Gibson was hailed as 'The Gold King', and some of his affluent friends, railroad men like Leland Stanford and Collis Huntington no less, convinced him to run for the United States Senate.

"Tall, thin, greying—oh, the devil cut quite a figure in Washington and out West, I can tell you. But no matter how distinguished he thought he'd become, the leopard can never change its spots. At a train station in Denver, now *Senator* J. Neil Gibson finally crossed paths with one of the men he thought he'd left behind in Hope Canyon, a tough old bird they called 'Boston'.

"As Kentuck told it, Boston was sitting on his haunches near the tracks eating a chicken bone and looking for an opportunity to hop on a carriage unseen. Just then, a group of well-dressed dignitaries strode onto the platform. At the center of the party beneath a silk top hat appeared a clean-shaven and familiar face. Many years had passed, but Boston said that no fake aristocratic smile could conceal the memory of Gibson's cruel eyes; and it took no time at all for Boston to get someone nearby to give him the man's name. Realizing that 'J. Neil' was in fact 'Jed Gibson', the old miner remembered how I hungered for news about the man; and as soon as the train departed, Boston was spending his last few coins on a telegram to Kentuck with word of his discovery.

"Kentuck admitted that it was against his better judgment to supply me with the name of my father. But Kentuck believed in Frontier Justice too and, knowing how badly I wanted to find the man, he gave the name to me anyhow. For over twenty years, I had tempered my vengeance; in others, the passion might have died out. But not in me, gentlemen. Not in *me!*" He raised a fist to emphasize his commitment. "Within hours, I gave notice to the officials at the bank in Sacramento where I'd been working, collected my belongings, and set out yet again to find my mother's killer.

"Only this time it wasn't difficult at all. I had to change my moniker, of course. 'Thomas Luck' would be familiar to anyone, like Jake Gibson himself, who knew Bret Harte's tale. For my new Christian name, I borrowed from a favourite playwright—though I dropped the final 'e'; for my surname, I took one that was common. Thanks to my banking experience and university degree, not only did 'Marlow Bates' quickly secure an accounting job in Senator Gibson's office, but it also didn't take him long to work his way up the ladder.

"For whatever the reason, not long after becoming

Senator, Gibson decided against seeking re-election. Perhaps he still suffered guilt over his murderous actions; perhaps he had some premonition that his past was about to overtake him. He'd had good fortune outside America before; he must have figured it was time to take his chances a second time, and so he left the country once again.

"Following Gibson's instructions, his agent purchased Thor Place, the old estate in Hampshire you've already seen; and the fugitive moved to England. In addition to his wife and children, a few handpicked members of his staff accompanied him to his new home. Myself included. I would have followed him anyway, but why shouldn't the meticulous 'Marlow Bates' have been selected to go along? Had I not provided useful service in maintaining the Senator's finances and investments? In point of fact, no sooner had we arrived in Hampshire than the fool appointed me manager of the new estate.

"At last, I possessed clear access to the fiend; unimpeded, I could implement my plan."

* * *

"From the start I had distractions. Maria Pinto—that is, Mrs. Gibson—always seemed to be hovering about. Despite her feminine charms, she served as an irritant to me. At least, at first. It was I whom the Senator trusted with the running of the estate, but that wasn't good enough for her. Oh, no. She made the inner workings of the household her private domain. I could settle great issues concerning revenues and taxes for the Senator; yet to appease his wife, I had to gain approval regarding the most inconsequential of expenditures—salt for the cook, paper for the governess.

"But don't be mistaken. Although Maria Gibson may have been close to fifty and no longer the young beauty that had first caught the Gold King's eye, she was still full of fire and quite 'handsome', as many a Brit described her over the years—though I should say that to my American ear, such a term stripped away the torrid passion that was her strongest allure.

"While long removed from Brazil, she continued to exude the tropics. Pouting or exulting whenever we discussed even the most trivial of issues, she seemed unable to contain her sultry nature. With her raven hair piled high above those soft shoulders, her voluptuous form slinking through the house, her dark skin pulsing, and her sharp eyes flashing, Maria Gibson epitomized the temptress, the seductress, the *femme fatale*."

Thomas Luck smiled and nodded at us. "I know what you're thinking, gentlemen, so let me say it for you—with her dark skin and black hair, Maria Gibson was the mirror image of my mother, my Cherokee mother. Oh, my father saw it too; and I have no doubt that is why Maria attracted him. Worse, the villain acted accordingly. I saw her bruises. I knew that he behaved in the same beast-like manner to his Maria as he had to his Sal.

"I suppose it proves that I am my father's son when I confess that eventually I too became intoxicated with Maria. Despite how much she vexed me, I looked forward to our meetings together, our promenades, our meals—in short, gentlemen—to any encounter that provided me the opportunity to inhale her bewitching fragrance, to look into her smouldering eyes—let alone to touch her soft hand or even brush up against her.

"To her everlasting credit, however, Maria had no interest in any man besides her husband. There was the irony. You see, *his* ardour had cooled while *hers* had intensified—a juxtaposition that made the brute's mistreatment of her all the sadder. I watched her bosom rise and fall when she dared approach him, and yet she had no place in her heart for me."

Luck drew back his shoulders now and lifted his chin. A more charitable reporter might describe his pose as heroic.

"Suddenly, it came to me," he announced. "Murdering *her* and blaming the death on her husband would epitomize poetic justice. It would also—or so I firmly hoped—exterminate my own desires that were beginning to drive me mad.

"But fate, as it often does, chose that moment to intervene and complicate matters. For just then, J. Neil Gibson, the master of Thor Place, hired the beautiful Grace Dunbar as governess, and I was forced to alter my plans.

"At first, I'd hoped to spend time with Grace myself. After all, we were both members of the same staff. Oh, I know what you're going to say—that thanks to my great responsibilities on the estate, I should rightly have considered myself *above* the social station of the general household; but my father's even loftier position never stopped *him* from mixing with those beneath him—at least, not when it was worth his while.

"I understood the way he operated, so I don't know why his pursuit of Grace surprised me. Thanks to her dark hair, sparkling eyes, and youthful nature, Grace Dunbar was a lot like my father's other women—at least, the two I knew of. Grace was more slender than Maria, more educated than my mother, and lighter in complexion than both; but from the obvious way my father fawned over her, I could see that his basic tastes hadn't changed much over the years. What's more, as governess to his children, Grace would remain under his roof every day.

"You don't have to be a genius to figure out that the estate *manager* was certainly no competition for the estate *owner*—even if the lord of the manor did happen to be married. The excessive flattering, the personal attention, the devoted glances—all seemed to pose no problem for her. I could tell from her radiant smiles, her childish laughter, her rich blushes, that she enjoyed spending time in his presence. I wasn't the only one watching this little dance, of course: Maria recognized Grace's appeal as well, and I'm sure that's why Maria hated her.

As much as I resented this budding relationship between my father and his children's governess, it didn't take long for me to appreciate the opportunities it presented. However much Grace might verbally deny her attraction to the Senator, I realized that her ever-increasing infatuation with the man was an emotion I could exploit. Thus, I bottled up my own feelings for Grace while encouraging her to talk with me, and so I learned how at bottom she truly feared my father's pursuit. She loved his two children and needed a salary, but she had reached the conclusion that her life would be far less complicated if she vacated her position.

"Needless to say, the Senator was not about to let her escape. If she would only consent to stay, he promised to leave her unmolested; he promised to regale her with money. In the end, he promised to give her whatever she wanted.

"I do believe that my father was actually surprised by how quickly Grace jumped at his final offer. I know *I* was. I encouraged her to do so, of course; but, you see, she's the type who champions all sorts of charities around the world. You know the causes I mean: food for the starving, work for the unemployed, money for the poor. 'Robber baron' he may have been, yet so great was the man's newfound love that he agreed to contribute to whatever benevolent societies Grace Dunbar paraded before him. He told anyone who'd listen that she had a 'heart of gold'. It's no exaggeration to say that people in every part of the globe profited from Miss Dunbar's peculiar relationship with my father. Everyone but me.

"I for one have never been concerned with the problems of the downtrodden. If I had any interest at all in the new Dunbar-Gibson commitment to saving humanity, it was only to what degree their relationship could provide *me* with the opportunity for crushing the man who'd killed my mother. And if I do say so myself, what a beautiful plan I envisioned!

"As I've said before, I had no interest in causing my father's death; that was too easy. My idea was far more ingenious. With but a single blow, I would deprive him of the two most meaningful women in his life; after all, he had deprived *me* of the most important one in mine.

"On the morning of that fateful day almost seven years ago, I easily arranged with Maria to meet me after dinner at Thor Bridge—something about a drainage issue I needed to show her. What's more, I told her that, since the problem might affect the health of the children, she should ask Miss Dunbar to join us. Well aware of their mutual dislike, I prompted Maria to get written confirmation from the governess agreeing to the time and place of the meeting. I warned Maria that I might be late, but that she should wait with Miss Dunbar for my appearance.

"The two women met as planned. At the same time, I was busy placing in Miss Dunbar's wardrobe the twin of the Smith and Wesson that I would use to shoot Maria Gibson. Both guns belonged to my father; and I had previously fired a single shot in the woods with one, so when that innocent weapon would later be found in the wardrobe, the police would believe it to be the gun responsible for Maria's murder. I'd also tied some strong twine around a heavy stone, which I'd earlier placed on the bridge behind a post of the balustrade. All that remained was to attach the other end of the twine to the butt of the pistol that I would bring along to my meeting with Maria, a sleight-of-hand I reckoned I could successfully accomplish once I'd reached the bridge.

"Good fortune smiled on me. For whatever the reason, by the time I reached the foot of the bridge, Maria was shouting at Grace. Knowing Maria's jealous temper, I wasn't surprised; nor could I have hoped for a better situation. I waited for Grace to run off—as I knew she would—and then I made my appearance. Maria was still enraged, and I begged a moment to lace my shoe. I was, of course, standing directly next to the spot where I'd earlier hidden the stone and string. After I'd turned my back and bent over, it was child's play to slip the gun out of my coat pocket and tie the free end of the twine around the gun's handle without being observed.

"'Calm down, Mrs. Gibson!' I called to Maria as I stood up, carefully concealing the gun in my coat pocket. 'Come here and let me show you the problem I told you about.'

"She caught her breath, wiped her eyes, and crossed her arms in front of her chest. Then she marched over to me. At the same time, with my left hand curled around the handle of the pocketed gun, I was able to manipulate the stone behind my back with my right hand and dangle it over the side of the bridge. When Maria reached me, I simply withdrew the pistol from my pocket and, ignoring the pull of the twine, placed the barrel against her right temple.

"For the merest instant, her eyes swelled with fear. Then, without so much as a single word, I squeezed the trigger and immediately released my hold on the gun. Once freed, the stone dutifully plunged into the water, dragging along the Smith and Wesson connected to it by the length of twine. To be sure, the gun nicked the wall, but the two splashes sounded almost like one.

"Good fortune smiled on me again. To my utter joy, Maria's dead hand still clutched the note Grace had sent confirming their meeting. All I had left to do was make my escape. The false evidence I'd planted in Grace Dunbar's wardrobe would incriminate her and send her to the gallows. And if it didn't? If I had made some sort of mistake and she wasn't accused? If the gun I used and the string and the stone were somehow discovered? If the pistol in the wardrobe was discovered to be a ploy? If? If? *If?* Why then, that little chip in the bridge—which I, of course, had no way of foreseeing—might convince even the cleverest of detectives—like you, Mr. Holmes—to fall for the dodge. You might just wrongly conclude that in committing suicide, the jealous wife had used the gun, the string, and the stone to frame her rival. At the very least, Maria would be dead, and Grace Dunbar's clandestine relationship with Gibson would be exposed. Either way, my father's life would be in shambles, and I could walk away a free man."

I shook my head. In concept, it seemed among the most diabolical plots that Holmes and I had ever encountered.

My friend sat grim-faced, no doubt still chastising himself for initially having fallen for Luck's ruse.

"Your visit to Baker Street all those years ago," Holmes charged the prisoner, "it was simply to establish this blind."

Luck grinned. "A rather clever manoeuvre to convince you not to believe Gibson's lies. He would say anything to gain your help in exonerating Grace Dunbar. As long as she appeared guilty, I had nothing to fear. It should have been the perfect crime."

"Save for the presence of Samuel Clemens." To Thomas Luck, Holmes' words must have sounded like simple fact. Only *I* knew how difficult it was even after all these years for Sherlock

Holmes to make such an admission.

Luck banged his fist on his cot. "Damn his eyes!" he roared. "He's the reason I had to escape from Thor Place—Clemens and his little trick with the glass that captured my finger-marks. He could have found them in my room, of course. But I'd been careless placing the pistol in the wardrobe. And when I saw that simple-minded policeman fish those two guns from the mere, I knew I'd been outsmarted."

"Where did you go?" asked Holmes calmly.

"Where did I go? I admit that I was afraid to leave the country. I figured the ports would be watched."

"They were."

"That's why I went inland," Luck grinned. "To the Cotswolds. Changed my name again. Got myself a job as a bookkeeper in Stow and stayed out of trouble."

"Ah, Watson," said Holmes recalling the note of warning received by the Senator at Thor Place. "The envelope was postmarked in Stow."

Thomas luck smiled for the first time. "It's a lovely little town, Stow-on-the-Wold. All those honey-coloured shops and houses. The River Windrush. The longer I remained there, the less I wanted to go back to America. And I didn't have to any more. But don't for a minute think I ever forgot Samuel Langhorne Clemens and all the trouble he'd caused me. I was in hiding thanks to him. And when I heard he was coming to Oxford, I figured it was my final chance at revenge."

"And so from Stow, you posted your threat against the so-called 'king'."

"The tip-off to my father? Yes. I figured he'd warn his old friend that someone was out to get him, and fear would become the appetizer to murder."

"And if the Senator didn't understand the quotation from Emerson? If he didn't connect 'King' to Clemens?"

Thomas Luck shrugged.

"You came very close this morning."

"Except for the fool who stepped between us."

"Your father," I said.

Thomas Luck issued a low laugh. "That's right. I killed m' dad. Sorry."

Holmes and I looked at each other.

"I should imagine we're finished here, Watson."

"What about *me*?" Luck demanded.

"You'll be sent to the Assizes. When your time in court is finished, I fancy you'll be hanged. And no one will hear any more about Thomas Luck."

"Not unless they read about the baby in Bret Harte's story, eh, Holmes?" I couldn't help offering. "Sales should go up with the news of Luck's hanging."

Seething at this final irony, Luck shut his eyes tight and balled both fists.

The summer sun previously fixed on the prisoner had shifted. With its brightness illuminating the rear of the cell, I could see now that the walls had been newly whitewashed. As yet, no writings graced the stones. Perhaps Luck would be the first occupant to scribble his outrage on the white plaster— though I had no reason to think he knew the German word for "revenge".

Holmes rapped on the door to summon the constable; but even after the policeman had locked the massive door behind us, we could still hear Luck shouting: "God damn you, Sherlock Holmes!"

As we were about to exit the station, Chief Inspector

Wheat handed Holmes a small, cream-coloured envelope. "This arrived when you were interrogating the prisoner."

Over Holmes' shoulder I saw the folded paper he'd slipped out from the envelope. The same colour as the cover, it was a sheet of hotel stationery. At the top were the printed words: *The Randolph Hotel, Beaumont Street, Oxford.* The message itself appeared short and neatly written, but I was too far away to read the script.

"It's from Mrs. Gibson," Holmes said. "She's with Clemens at the Randolph and would like us to join them."

"My God Holmes," I said softly. "What a time the poor woman has had of it."

A hansom stood at the kerb, prepared to convey us the short distance to Beaumont Street.

Chapter Sixteen

Loyalty to a petrified opinion
never yet broke a chain or freed a human soul.
--Mark Twain
"Consistency" (speech, essay)

The honey-coloured bricks of the Randolph were glowing red in the afternoon sun when Holmes and I arrived in Beaumont Street. The hotel itself is a staid and proper five-storey Victorian with high-pitched roof and lancet shaped windows, yet today the grey pavement in front of its entrance was ringed with cheering celebrity-seekers hoping for a glimpse of Samuel Clemens.

Their jubilant anticipation jarred with the gravity of the day. The horrific murder of Jed Gibson had poisoned any sense of accomplishment accompanying the arrest of Thomas Luck. And now we were to face not only Gibson's widow but also Samuel Clemens, whose antagonism towards Holmes still rankled. Having to push our way through the crowd didn't make the meeting any easier.

And even then we weren't home free. For after entering the building, we discovered that in spite of the best intentions of the hotel clerks and managers, a group of gawkers and photographers had somehow slipped into the lobby to get one last look at the famed American writer. Only after much pleading, coaxing, and shooing by the staff did the intruders finally leave.

As I've already reported, death was no stranger to Samuel Clemens.   He'd already buried his beloved wife, his eldest daughter, and an infant son; and he knew how to carry on. In truth, the gunfire that had killed his close friend was so quick and the seventy-two-year-old Clemens no longer so spry that, thanks to the resolve of Kipling and others nearby in the procession, I believe the writer never fully grasped all that had taken place as he turned towards the gates of the Sheldonian. At least, I hope so.

I'm not certain when Clemens was actually told of the tragedy. His secretary, Ralph Ashcroft, had been waiting for him inside the Sheldonian and hadn't witnessed the shooting itself. I did learn from the pressmen who followed his every move that once the encænia had ended, a large, cheering crowd escorted Clemens down Catte Street to the gates of All Souls College and that for the rest of the afternoon Clemens kept to the schedule that the Oxford administrators had prepared for him.

He appeared in the library at All Souls where the Chancellor's luncheon celebrating the honourees took place. The band of the 2nd V.B. Oxfordshire Light Infantry provided music from the lawn of the Great Quadrangle. Later, Clemens joined other dignitaries at an informal garden party sponsored by the president of St. John's. Also accompanied by a military band, this affair was held under a large tent in the Groves and in the cloisters.

Now Sam Clemens was sitting along side Grace Gibson on a grey-corduroy couch in the far corner of the Randolph's large sitting room. Judging from his grave expression, I sensed that the day's tragic developments must have submerged most of the elation. Clemens was dressed in his classic white serge suit, white shirt, and white cravat. His attire created so serene—dare I say "saintly"?—an appearance that it was hard to take one's eyes off of him. Looking at Clemens like that, I was put in mind of the occasion seven years before at Dollis Hill House when he'd spoken so enviously of how it is the *white* cat that always gets the attention.

Although much less dramatic, Grace Gibson was also dressed in white, having changed from the morning frock of powder blue that had been soaked with her husband's blood.

Holmes and I approached the pair.

"Our condolences, Mrs. Gibson," Holmes offered with a bow of his head.

"I didn't bring along a black dress," said Mrs. Gibson softly. "I never thought I'd have the need."

Holmes and I quickly drew up two chairs.

"Quite a day," Sam Clemens sighed. Twenty-four hours before, he was the happiest man on the planet anticipating his honorary degree; now, he was looking his age: the lines crossing his pale face seemed deeper; his dishevelled white locks stood out in all directions, his cheeks appeared hollow, his lips turned down.

"I would have travelled the seven seas," Clemens said, "for the degree I received this morning at that fine old theatre. It is the greatest honour that has ever fallen to me. Not to mention the celebrations that have accompanied it—the luncheons, the receptions, the dinners."

"You're well deserving," said I, stating the obvious.

"And I'm not finished *yet*," Clemens insisted. "There's so much going on! Why, just for this meeting alone, I had to bow out of what you people call a 'gaudy' at Christ Church. I was supposed to be sitting at the high table with the big shots—the Chancellor, the heads of college, and Ambassador Reid. Given all that's happened today, they granted me permission to skip the meal—as long as I promised to be there no later than 8:00 when the speeches are set to begin."

"Jed would have wanted you to go," said Mrs. Gibson. "I can manage, and the governess is watching the children."

Sam Clemens slowly shook his head, his expressive brows knit. "You know that I would return my degree and all the hoopla that goes along with it if I could restore my old friend to life."

Mrs. Gibson took Clemens' hand in hers and squeezed it. Tears welled in her eyes.

As best he could, Holmes summarized for the two of them all that we'd learned from Thomas Luck's confession.

"Neil had changed so much," Grace Gibson said. "I thought I knew all the stories of his past life in California. He told them to me himself—though not every one of them I now see. He'd obviously been a horror as a younger man, but I must believe, gentlemen, that our years together had tempered him."

"Today," Sam Clemens said of his friend, "Jed was a real hero. In my mind, he shall forever be remembered as the man who saved my life—stepping in front of that lunatic with the gun like he did. I will not allow him to be dismissed as some sort of beast who murdered a woman and drove her poor boy—his own son—mad. That's in the distant past; today he is much more."

We all sat silent for a bit, pondering Clemens' words. A few whines from the exiting crowd still hung in the air.

"What happens now, Mr. Holmes?" Grace Gibson asked at last.

"The police will keep your husband's body for the autopsy. There will be an inquest; but with all the attendant witnesses, that should be a mere formality. Then they will release the body to you for the funeral, which, I imagine, you'd want to take place in Hampshire."

She nodded, and then silence reigned again.

This time it was Sherlock Holmes who broke it. He rose slowly and turned to address Sam Clemens.

"Mr. Clemens," he offered, "in some unholy way, I seem to have been acting much like the very villain to whom Dr. Watson and I listened this entire afternoon—a madman driven by revenge."

Clemens' massive eyebrows rose at this strange admission.

"You see," said Holmes, "like Luck, I too have harbored a grudge for many years. Too many. It is time to start anew. The story you wrote about me—"

"Let *me* say it first, Mr. Holmes," Clemens interrupted. "I'm sorry I ripped you. My pride was injured when I discovered that all my detective work had been left out of Dr. Watson's report."

"But—" I was once again going to point out the role of Conan Doyle.

"*Enough!*" Clemens cried. "In memory of Jed Gibson, let's bury the hatchet, shall we?" Then he turned to me. "I might even go so far as to pay *you* a compliment, Doctor. If I hadn't first read *your* narrative about the murder at Lauriston Gardens, I could never have written *my* little tale about revenge. No doubt you noticed how the demand for vengeance moved my plot just as it had driven yours in *A Study in Scarlet*—not to mention our similar encounters with the word 'Rache' on a wall. And that bit about my detective whose sense of smell could sniff out the guilty party? Why, I simply made literal your metaphor about "human bloodhounds". Actually, Dr. Watson, I really am quite indebted to you."

I'm afraid my blush revealed that, in spite of all the talk of hurt feelings and revenge, I could still value a compliment from Samuel Clemens as much as I did the first day I met him at the Turkish baths. "Thank you," was all I could muster.

Sherlock Holmes extended his hand to the man in white; and Clemens, relying for support on the arm of the couch, stood up to face him.

"Mr. Clemens," Holmes proclaimed, "you're an excellent detective. Let us not forget that Scotland Yard has only now come round to creating the fingerprint bureau you envisioned years ago. Well before the Yard did, you understood the importance of such evidence; you recognized what it took the professionals years to comprehend."

Clemens raised his shaggy eyebrows again and looked at Mrs. Gibson and then at me. Pulling at his dark moustache, he turned back to my friend. "Mr. Holmes," said he, "I can think of no finer source from whom to receive such a compliment."

We nodded our good-byes then, and Holmes and I left Mrs. Gibson and Sam Clemens alone together in the lobby of the Randolph.

"Come, Watson," said Holmes. "Let us return to London."

The local newspapers attempted to conceal as much of the shooting as possible from the American pressmen who were following Mark Twain's triumphant visit to Oxford. But word of the murder of Jed Gibson and the attempted murder of Samuel Clemens got out. How else to interpret the story that appeared in the *New York Times* on 30 June 1907? Noting that Clemens had slept till noon on the day after receiving his Oxford degree, the report described him as "not disposed to banter or indulge in any quips." "He was a changed man," the *Times* said, "quite different from the Mark Twain who had cracked jokes at the Pilgrims' luncheon two days before. He was excessively solemn even for an American humorist off duty."

* * *

Holmes and I found ourselves alone in our railway compartment during the return to Paddington.

"It was a case full of ironies, Holmes," I observed with a shrug. "Senator Gibson had everything. Now he's dead. The crazed killer who spent years nurturing his hatred came close to perfecting his deranged plan. Now he's facing the rope."

Sherlock Holmes smiled wryly and stretched out his long legs. "Perhaps," said he, "the late Bret Harte should have the final word about this case, Watson. After all, it was he who famously said, "The only sure thing about luck is that it will change."

That was the last comment Holmes made to me before nodding off. Since the start of our all-night vigil at the Sheldonian, it had been a long day. Lulled by the rhythm of the wheels and the pitching of the carriage, I too shut my eyes.

Suddenly, the train whistle shrieked, and I started. It would be the final cry in a winding tale so full of vengeance and—literary diversions notwithstanding—so little joy.

THE END

Editor's Suggested Reading

For those seeking further understanding of the events chronicled by Doctor Watson, I suggest beginning with the primary sources referred to in the narrative: Dr. Watson's "The Problem of Thor Bridge," Mark Twain's "A Double-Barrelled Detective Story," and Bret Harte's "The Luck of Roaring Camp" and "The Stolen Cigar Case."

For additional biographical information, the third volume of Mark Twain's *Autobiography* recently published by the University of California Press is an excellent place to start. *Mark Twain: The Complete Interviews* edited by Gary Scharnhorst provides lots of details related to Clemens' trips to England, as do Howard D. Baetzhold's *Mark Twain and John Bull: The British Connection* and Edward Connery Lathem's *Mark Twain's Four Weeks in England 1907*. For content directly related to Clemens' stay in Dollis Hill House, see Hamilton Hay's booklet, *Summer in Paradise*.

As far as specific literary analysis is concerned, a number of scholars have discussed Clemens' connections with crime fiction. See James Ritunnano's "Mark Twain vs. Arthur Conan Doyle on Detective Fiction" in the *Mark Twain Journal* (Winter 1971). The previously mentioned *Mark Twain and John Bull* contains an informative discussion of "A Double-Barrelled Detective Story." In addition to the title story and two others, the Oxford Mark Twain volume entitled *The Stolen White Elephant and Other Detective Stories* contains two relevant essays regarding Clemens and mystery fiction: Walter Mosley's "Reflections on the Detective Stories of Mark Twain and an Idea or Two More About His Fiction" and Lillian S. Robinson's "For Further Reading."

Finally, for commentary regarding the discovery of the word *Rache* on various walls, see "*Rache* is the German for Revenge" by Maria Von Krebs in *The Baker Street Journal* of January 1960.

D.D.V.

Also from MX Publishing

MX Publishing is the world's largest specialist Sherlock Holmes publisher, with over a hundred titles and fifty authors creating the latest in Sherlock Holmes fiction and non-fiction.

From traditional short stories and novels to travel guides and quiz books, MX Publishing cater for all Holmes fans.

The collection includes leading titles such as _Benedict Cumberbatch In Transition_ and _The Norwood Author_ which won the 2011 Howlett Award (Sherlock Holmes Book of the Year).

MX Publishing also has one of the largest communities of Holmes fans on _Facebook_ with regular contributions from dozens of authors.

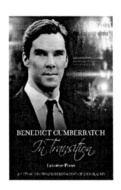

www.mxpublishing.com

223

Also from MX Publishing

"Phil Growick's, 'The Secret Journal of Dr Watson', is an adventure which takes place in the latter part of Holmes and Watson's lives. They are entrusted by HM Government (although not officially) and the King no less to undertake a rescue mission to save the Romanovs, Russia's Royal family from a grisly end at the hand of the Bolsheviks. There is a wealth of detail in the story but not so much as would detract us from the enjoyment of the story. Espionage, counter-espionage, the ace of spies himself, double-agents, double-crossers...all these flit across the pages in a realistic and exciting way. All the characters are extremely well-drawn and Mr Growick, most importantly, does not falter with a very good ear for Holmesian dialogue indeed. Highly recommended. A five-star effort."
The Baker Street Society

Also from MX Publishing

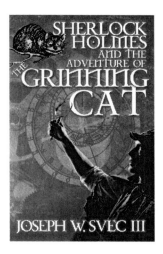

Sherlock Holmes and The Adventure of The Grinning Cat

"Joseph Svec, III is brilliant in entwining two endearing and enduring classics of literature, blending the factual with the fantastical; the playful with the pensive; and the mischievous with the mysterious. We shall, all of us young and old, benefit with a cup of tea, a tranquil afternoon, and a copy of Sherlock Holmes, The Adventure of the Grinning Cat."
Amador County Holmes Hounds Sherlockian Society

Lightning Source UK Ltd.
Milton Keynes UK
UKOW02f0117250416

272905UK00002B/19/P